The room had become no more than background for Liz. Sally looked at the old stand-up radiator in front of the window, thinking that in winter, heat would rise off it in waves that changed everything beyond it. Lifting the violet and running it across her own cheek, she wondered if Liz was feeling what she was feeling. Or did Liz think she was a bore? And what made it like this? Why Liz? Why this room, this city, this day? Did love, like heat, rise because it had to?

She replaced the violet, her fingertips dipping into the goblet, coming out dripping. "Liz," she said, not meaning to.

"Sally," said Liz and Sally looked at her startled, like a deer surprised against the snow.

Liz's dark eyes burned behind her glasses. Her mouth—could it be swollen in anticipation?

Sally stood, walked carefully around the glass coffee table as if it were a frozen pond she might fall into. It seemed to take forever to clear. Then she folded her long legs, and dropped on top of them.

She sat facing Liz, afraid to draw breath because it might be a groan. Liz swayed toward her, head down, long dark hair hanging, her body swaying tentatively. . . .

HOME
IN
YOUR
HANDS

HOME IN YOUR HANDS

by
Lee Lynch

the NAIAD PRESS inc.
1986

Printed in the United States of America
First Edition

Cover design by Tee A. Corinne
Typesetting by Sandi Stancil
Edited by Katherine V. Forrest

The poem "Pallas on page vii is from H.D., *Selected Poems*. Copyright © 1957 by Normal Holmes Pearson. Reprinted by permission of New Directions Publishing Corporation.

Library of Congress Cataloging-in-Publication Data

Lynch, Lee, 1945—
    Home in your hands.

    1. Lesbians—Fiction.   I. Title.
PS3562.Y426H6 1986   813'.54   86-12762
ISBN 0-930044-80-0

For

Tee A. Corinne

Ah, could they know
how violets throw strange fire,
red and purple and gold,
how they glow
gold and purple and red
where her feet tread.

H.D.
from "Pallas"

WORKS BY LEE LYNCH

CREDITS

Dutch and Sybil I appeared in *Common Lives/Lesbian Lives*, 12/83.
Dusty Eats Out appeared in *On Our Backs*, Winter, 1986.
Marie-Christine II appeared in *On Our Backs*, Fall, 1985.
At A Bar VI: Winter Sun, appeared in *Common Lives/Lesbian Lives*, Fall, 1985.

ACKNOWLEDGEMENTS

With thanks to everyone, mentioned and unmentioned, who gave something of themselves to this book: Carol Seajay, Deb Pascale, Katherine Forrest, The Southern Oregon Women Writers' Group, The Bloodroot Collective, Debra Scionti, Bill D. and Sue Cox.

And to honor the memory of June Nolan who, more than most of us, couldn't live without love.

CONTENTS

JEFFERSON I:
HOME IN YOUR HANDS

— 1 —

Jefferson stood naked, feeling strong and powerful. The curtains of her dormitory window were parted slightly so that she could see the morning beyond them. The fall light was golden, the day so intensely clear that everything shone with the remnants of the night's moisture. A few cars out early Saturday could be heard below on the street. In the suburbs of New York leaves would be burning; here in the city chestnuts roasted all up and down the avenues. Was it possible winter wouldn't come this year? The city seemed to waver before her eyes, so magical, so full of promising corners and storefronts and signs she felt confused and excited at all the choices, like riches, before her.

A day to celebrate, she thought, full of her joy, her youth, her powers. She jogged down the hall to the communal bathroom. It smelled of mint toothpastes and disinfectant. The tile floor of the shower stall was cold on her bare feet, but she bore this discomfort stoically, like all others. Under a sharp hot spray she lathered and shampooed her athlete's body vigorously, roughly, from short hair to well-fleshed but neatly formed breasts, to solid muscled legs.

"Jefferson!"

Ginger's voice. Four years after they'd become lovers it still filled her with a warmth as steamy as the shower. The continued to spend hours in each other's arms imagining their lives together after graduation. Ginger planned to pursue a career in dance, Jefferson to get a Master's Degree in Physical Education.

Over and over she dwelt on how perfect Ginger was for her, how lucky she was to have found her. But then at times she'd feel frightened at how irritable she could be with Ginger, and by her own nearly compulsive flings with other women. Today she felt so good she only chuckled. Marriage would cure her of those urges, she was sure of it.

She turned the shower off. "This is going to be one damn fine day, Ginge."

She could hear Ginger's toothbrush.

"You want to climb the Empire State Building with me?" Jefferson called out. "Or how about taking a boat trip around Manhattan?" Dry, robed, she joined Ginger at the sinks. "What a *face*," she told her. "*I* know, we'll go to the Park and I'll count your freckles."

Ginger smiled broadly at her in the mirror, blue eyes filled with light. "Again?" she teased affectionately.

"I didn't finish last time." Her spirits were so high she wanted to bounce up and down. Shoot baskets into the toilet booths. Surely her blood carbonated with excitement as it coursed through her body. It'd take a lot of wine to even her out this day. She wished she could hug Ginger hard, but they'd be drummed out of the P.E. Department in an hour if they got caught.

Ginger turned to her, brushing her shoulder-length coppery hair, a long-fingered hand curved around her brush. The touch of those hands was a gift Jefferson had found in no other woman. Ginger shook her head, eyes amused and sad. "You've forgotten mid-term exams are next week."

She had. "Hell, we're seniors. Seniors don't have to study." She kept smiling, and began to clip the nails on her own solid and capable looking hands. She didn't want Ginger to worry about her grades, didn't want Ginger to leave her thinking she was no good, but damn, last night was to have been the final party before she buckled down. She had to get her grade point average up this semester if she wanted to graduate on time.

"We'll make it fun, Jeff. We can go study in the park. I'll help you."

"No baby, you have your own work to do. I'll get by. I always do." She gave Ginger her most reassuring, charming smile.

Ginger, from a working class Bronx family, had come to college with hardly an ounce of self-confidence. Jefferson, who'd grown up with well-to-do parents in Westchester County, had learned to exude confidence and prosperity whether she felt them or not. And she knew her own self-possession always reassured Ginger.

Half an hour later Ginger was in Jefferson's room. Jefferson pulled her close and they held. Always, Jefferson thought, hands firmly, familiarly caressing Ginger, the touch of this woman was like winning the World Series. "You take my breath away," she told her.

Ginger moved her face for a kiss and replied, "I love you."

"Open the window," Jefferson urged, reluctantly letting her go. "Tell me you can resist a day like this."

Ginger pressed her forehead against the screen while Jefferson admired her profile. She could see Ginger take a deep breath of the air. "It's gorgeous."

"Your accent's showing," she said, moving to Ginger.

The occasional harshness that remained in Ginger's accent grated on Jefferson, who'd been raised to sound like a class, not a location, but she thought she was good at keeping the irritation from her criticism. Ginger wanted to succeed out there in the world, after all.

"Sorry," said Ginger quickly, trying again. "Gorgeous," she repeated, this time in open tones.

A warm breeze seemed to swirl into the room and wrap around them both. Jefferson had dressed in a faintly pink oxford-cloth shirt, a white v-neck sweater, sharply-pressed white slacks and white moccasins. She stepped behind Ginger and pressed herself full-length to her back, reaching around to cup her breasts. "We could go out to Long Island Sound and rent a sailboat."

Ginger turned and moved her eyes down her lover's body. "You're too irresistible, that's the problem."

"Am I pressuring you, baby?" she asked. "I thought it would be something *you'd* like to do."

"It would, Jeff. I'm just not convinced it's a good idea this weekend."

"We won't go," she said, disappointed—crushed—but unwilling to upset Ginger.

"Oh, Jeff. Does it mean that much to you?"

Jefferson slumped, body and mind swallowed by depression. She lay her head on Ginger's shoulder. "Not if you're going to worry all day."

"You feel so small when you're sad," said Ginger, her tone remorseful, her arms comforting, her hands, those magical hands, soothing.

Jefferson snuggled against the beloved body, feeling momentarily safe and free from her own demanding will.

"I wouldn't worry all day," said Ginger.

Jefferson straightened, still holding her. "You mean you'll take a holiday with me?"

"I didn't *say* that," Ginger warned with a laugh. "I don't want you thinking you can wrap me around your little finger."

She began to weakly twist away from Jefferson. They fought playfully, then fell laughing onto the unmade bed.

Jefferson's good cheer returned and she knew that Ginger would spend the day with her. But *was* this so important? More important than grades and Ginger's peace of mind? They tussled more. How many days like this did one woman get in a lifetime, she asked herself, convinced again that it was the right thing for both of them. She could feel Ginger's gentle fingers in her still-wet hair, her lips soft, nibbling, biting her own lips, tasting like mint.

"Will you play hookey with me?"

"Lock the door," came Ginger's husky answer.

"Will you?" she repeated after she'd come back. She knelt at the edge of the bed, Ginger's feet against her shoulders, and rubbed her cheeks along those soft inner thighs. "I could die happy here," she said.

"Not quite yet," Ginger whispered, rubbing back against her. "Not till you finish what you started."

Her lips pressed against Ginger's hair, still moistly hot from a shower. She parted it slowly with her tongue, then asked against her, "Will you?"

"Ohh, I like that," said Ginger, pressing back. "But Jeff, I want to graduate with a three point five . . ."

"I'll give you a four point oh . . ."

"Oh, Jefferson, oh." Ginger cleared her throat as if to gain control of herself. "I'm not majoring in sex."

"You should. You're real good, baby."

She loved Ginger's mild taste. No matter how many girls she went out with on the sly, her moral code insisted that she only go down on Ginger. If Ginger ever found out about the others, maybe it wouldn't hurt as much.

As Ginger's thighs hugged her head she pictured herself, this beautiful woman proudly on her arm, standing on the sidelines of a field hockey game. Her old team would be more spirited because she, a school hero, watched. Ginger would be happy and secure, holding her hand. Always, Ginger had liked visiting with the coach and teachers, liked being her girl where that counted most. . . . And Jefferson, all in white, a white crock of wine in her hand, would feel that mellow high only Saturday afternoons on a playing field and a few drinks could give her. . . .

She remembered Taffy, that cute little senior from her old prep school who'd always been especially attentive. Would Taffy be around if there was a game today?

She rose, fell, with Ginger's hips, her tongue no longer roving, but strumming the slick full flesh, over and over on the same spot. She'd check the schedule and they'd drive up there. Ginger would have a great time. She'd make sure of that.

— 2 —

In the suburban Westchester County town north of New York City where Jefferson's old team was scheduled to play that day, the golden light was softer and spread a romantic haze over the oranges, reds and yellows of the trees, over the bleached light greens of the playing field, and over the young women in short plaid skirts, intent on their game. Jefferson filled her chest with balmy air which did, indeed, carry on it the scent of dozens of backyard leaf-piles gloriously, briefly, blazing. The thwack of the girls' wooden hockey sticks as they clashed defending their goals was a sound which stirred her more than prayers or anthems. *This* was winterless fall, this was sweet nostalgia, this was living at its best.

"Having a good time?" she asked Ginger, her heart joy-filled.

"I love sharing this part of your life." Ginger's face was flushed, her absorption in the game obvious.

"Want to come back to the parking lot with me?"

"Jeff, don't you care that your team is losing?" Ginger clapped as the Bluejays made a goal, and cheered with the other bystanders. The coach, an old classmate of Jefferson's, ran to hug the scorer.

Jefferson watched the players a few more minutes. They seemed distanced by the hazy light, as if they were floating back and forth across the field. This could all be a pleasant dream. How could she explain to Ginge that it wasn't the winning, the losing, or even the playing? It was the feeling of well-being which was important. The ease of a day blessed by such indulgent light that she felt free of the strictures any normal day would bring. Wasn't it like getting drunk? Life stopped being so hard.

She strode toward the parking lot in her whites. Inside the station wagon she'd borrowed from her parents were a picnic basket and supplies. Before leaving the city she and Ginger had stocked the car with rolls, cold meats, a cooler full of soda, a cheesecake and three white crocks of wine. She lowered the car's tailgate and pulled the second bottle from its hiding place. This was not an Ivy League football game, and tailgating, especially with drinking, was not a custom. But she'd thought it would please Ginger to invite the team for a snack after the game. And the teachers were always glad for some convivial bourbon to pour into their cups of soda.

"Hi, Taffy," she said, lounging against the car with her white bottle.

The girl reached for the bottle. The team manager, she wore her short-skirted uniform like cheerleader garb. She fell, laughing, against Jefferson's chest as she wrestled for the bottle. Jefferson felt a stab of regret at the four impassable years between them. But it didn't matter anyway. I know right from wrong, she reminded herself. I have a will of my own. Sometimes she seemed compelled to do crazy things, but she wouldn't let herself today. This would be a perfect day for Ginger.

"I'm eighteen, Jeffy, honest."

"Since when? And *don't* call me Jeffy." It was a nickname which seemed to have come naturally to the prep school crowd and she was still trying to get rid of it.

"Since last week. I started school late."

"Looks like everything else was on time," she commented in a wry tone, surveying the body bursting with adolescence. A few years from now the girl would still be pretty, but nothing like this—the shoulder-length bouncing hair, the breasts newly full, the face without makeup. And she spoke easily, in Jefferson's unaccented tones. They could have been raised in the same family. Jefferson gave in, handed over the bottle.

"Thanks, sport," said Taffy, and drank.

They sat and talked, legs dangling from the tailgate. Jefferson felt, with the cheering and wood against wood sounds farther away, as if she were even deeper into a dream. There wasn't any harm, surely, in flirting with this kid?

"I really thought Jody would break your record this year, Jeffy."

Jefferson tried not to show her pride that no one had

scored more goals in one game than she, and moved to lean her back against the inside of the wagon, aware of her pose as she raised her knees and held the white crock between them, her gold I.D. bracelet hanging loosely from one wrist, on the other an expandable watch band glinting in the sun. "You have new teachers, a new coach. It takes time."

Taffy reached for the bottle again.

"I don't want to get you in trouble," said Jefferson, withholding it as Taffy's small hands played at prying hers off. She should have bought more.

"I have gum to cover the smell," scoffed Taffy.

She surrendered the bottle. There were plenty of liquor stores nearby. "You look too young to be drinking."

"I started when I was fourteen."

She clucked her tongue against the roof of her mouth, trying to be disapproving. "Me too," she admitted with a smile, frankly proud of her precocity. "What else did you start at fourteen?"

Taffy threw back her head and laughed. "Don't tell me you mean *boys*. I only go with them to please Mom and Dad."

Their eyes held. It seemed to Jefferson as if the worshipful little girl in Taffy was doing battle with the seductive woman. She knew the woman had won out when she felt lured by her gaze. She tried, for a while, not to look at Taffy's breasts, or her swinging, nearly naked legs, not to touch, with her unquiet hands, the young siren body.

Ginger joined them. It was the end of the game. All three worked to set out the food.

"Why don't you two stay up here tonight?" suggested Taffy. "I'm going to a bar with a bunch of the kids."

"A bar, eh?" repeated Jefferson, a vision of a long night's laughter and dancing forming in her mind. Then too, she thought, hardly conscious that it was a motive, she wouldn't have to come down from her high.

Taffy's eyes narrowed challengingly above her raised chin. "You've heard of the Cliffs?"

Jefferson shot a quick look at Taffy, trying to hide and at the same time reveal a knowing grin. The White Cliffs had been a gay bar when she was in school. So Taffy *was* out. Still she fought with herself against strengthening their tie, against announcing herself as available by acknowledging, out loud, that she was gay. Oh, everyone knew it, but it seemed to be one of those unwritten lesbian rules that the minute you admitted it, you might as well disrobe and hold out your arms. For herself, coming out to another woman was an intimate revelation, sometimes a sexual response.

Rather than make the hard decision, she found herself saying, "I guess it wouldn't matter whether we went back tonight or in the morning." Besides, she could always back out by playing dumb when they got to the Cliffs, she thought, knowing—while pretending to herself not to—that her pride would never allow that even if the bartender didn't happen to remember her. "What do you think, Ginge?"

While Ginger hesitated, alternating slices of cheese with meat, Taffy said, "You could stay at my parents' place. I'll go call mother and tell her you'll be there for dinner. She's been asking to meet you, Jefferson."

She noted that Taffy hadn't called her Jeffy in front of Ginger.

"My famous girlfriend," laughed Ginger, looking adoringly toward Jefferson as Taffy had. She fastened the leather thong which held her hair, never taking her eyes from Jefferson, and raised her eyebrows questioningly.

Jefferson stood relaxed, legs apart, arms folded. She wanted to show that she cared nothing for Ginger's decision. But she was fervently hoping to extend this glowing day. Her mouth tasted brackish with old wine and she reached for the bottle.

Ginger spoke. "All right, Taffy." She told Jefferson,

"As long as we start back to the city early."

"Today's shot anyway," Jefferson replied nonchalantly, her heart alive again with excitement. "We might as well stay. Unless you'd rather go home."

Ginger leaned toward her, resting one delicate hand lightly on her forearm. The smell of burning leaves mingled with Ginger's scent, both smells warm and familiar in the afternoon sun. Ginger whispered, "I'm only home in your hands."

"Thank God," Jefferson replied, love surging in her.

Taffy leapt up and hugged Jefferson, and then, as if an afterthought, hugged Ginger too. Jefferson watched the two of them: the smaller, alluring Taffy, the back of her thighs showing as she stretched up to Ginger; the tall, almost statuesque redhead, gracefully, lightly, holding the girl. No comparison, she thought, smiling into Ginger's eyes, full of the warmth Ginger induced in her, certain that this was the woman for her. There is no way I'm going to lose that gem to some good-time kid who wants me for a notch in her belt.

She tipped a quick shot of bourbon into a cup of Coke; then, unthinking, she tipped it again.

— 3 —

The early winter dark came as a shock to Jefferson. She stood with Taffy on the porch while Taffy smoked a cigarette. But for the black chill through a light jacket, she felt dulled by a cocktail and wine with dinner on top of the afternoon's drinking. Ginger was inside watching a TV ballet with Taffy's parents. Out here high hedges obscured all but hints of neighboring lights. She felt enclosed. Her skin crawled. A blueness, the last sign of light from her perfect day, seemed to seep out of the night, into her. Would it never be time to go to the bar?

She sat heavily on a hanging wicker love seat.

"What's the matter, Jeffy?" asked Taffy, sitting beside her. Taffy had changed to tight cuffed jeans, a white shirt open at the throat, and a madras jacket.

They swung gently.

She sighed after a while and, looking across the yard, spoke to the hedges, to the specks of light that promised a world beyond her blues. "The day's over, that's all. I got up and the world promised me something. It staged a spectacular: trumpets, dancing girls, glitter and song. But it was a sham. Look—the curtain's down and it's gone, every bit of it." She held out empty hands.

Taffy took one hand and laid it palm up across her own. She began to play with the fingers, to trace the lines of the palm. "No one with hands as beautiful as yours should feel bad," Taffy said. "Look how strong, how sensitive. I'll bet Ginger loves these hands."

A little thrill of pleasure pierced her fog. She was still so numb she ignored the sentry voice inside her, warning, warning of this beckoning stranger Taffy. But Jefferson would do anything to lift her heavy mood.

"Every day's like that, Taffy. You wake up full of purpose, thinking this will be the day, and it ends, and it wasn't. Someday I'll have been shot down so often I won't even feel the excitement any more."

Taffy's face looked like the hockey players' had, so intent on winning that no emotion showed. Nor was there a note of concern in her voice when she asked, "The day for what?"

"Maybe if I knew that, I'd find it."

"Find what?" persisted Taffy.

"I want to say fame, fortune, success. But I know I don't want to work that hard. The only thing I really long for is something called home. An end to the road, the quest, the tension of the search."

"*I* can't wait to get *away* from home."

"That's just the problem. I'm always trying to get away from what I think of as home too. Why do I feel so excited when I think I'm there, then lose interest?"

"What are you *talking* about, Jeffy? Ginger?"

Jefferson looked down at her hands, at Taffy's small fingernails, daintily shaped and polished, ever-moving across her own. How could these big hands ever make a home for Ginger when they were so restless, so uncontrolled themselves? What was wrong with her? She closed her hand on Taffy's without considering consequences, just to see how it felt.

"Jeffy, Jeffy," said the girl in a low purring voice. "I *knew* you wanted me."

"But—"

Taffy had pushed Jefferson back and lay half on top of her, her lips passionately assaulting Jefferson's.

"But I don't—" She hesitated to reject Taffy, not wanting the girl to dislike her and, as well, not wanting to act in a way that would confirm that they'd been flirting.

"Shh, Jeffy. I know." The girl rubbed her breasts against Jefferson. "Ginger's right inside. I don't want to see *you* in trouble either." Taffy moved off her and sat upright. "Wasn't I smart? I didn't wear any lipstick even though I longed to look great for you."

She knew the sparkle in Taffy's eyes. The animation bred from winning. And certainly the touch of her breasts had been exciting. "But—" she began once more when Ginger, with her graceful, spirited walk, came out onto the porch.

She stood to greet Ginger, saved from her own wavering impulses. "I need to stop at a liquor store on the way," she said, cheered by the feeling of escape, by the rush of adrenalin Taffy's advances and Ginger's arrival had stirred.

She drove, and bought more wine and soon afterward filled the station wagon with half the hockey team. They flew through the clear star-sparkling night to the bar where once again there was promise in the air thick as the cigarette smoke. Jefferson talked and laughed boisterously with everyone. She kept close to Ginger, brought her drinks, danced with her, brashly elbowed a path to the bathroom for her.

She was raucous, even overbearing, and tried to quiet herself, to assume the air of a dignified alumni. But she was rushing to get somewhere and she shouted, and drank, to drown out the space between here and there.

Then, all at once, she'd arrived. The golden day had returned. Life was hard no longer. She moved with ease, laughed low and talked quietly, with an air of amused tolerance.

Taffy came to the table, eyes glittering like the loud jukebox. "May I dance with your girlfriend?" she asked Ginger.

Jefferson saw Ginger—dear, trusting Ginger—assent.

"No," she said herself, one hand closing around Ginger's where it lay on the table. Her lips seemed to burn from Taffy's earlier kiss. "I'm home." It sounded, of course, as if she meant being close to Ginger. But really she was talking about the state just short of unconsciousness, where one movement sends the drunk toppling from her chair, from her peace, from the weight of her passions and will.

"Time to go, Jeff," said Ginger a moment, or hours, later.

She leaned heavily on Ginger as they went to the car. Someone handed them coffee.

"Can you drive?" whispered Ginger.

In answer Jefferson recklessly kissed her full on the mouth.

A chorus of wolf-calls came from the back of the wagon. Jefferson began to drive smoothly, fearlessly, a lopsided grin on her face, back to Taffy's town.

Once she'd delivered the tired gang, she drove back to the hedge-walled house. At the sight of it her blues returned.

Taffy showed them to a room. "Sorry about the single beds," she said.

They undressed in the dark, each collapsing into her own bed.

"I love you, Jeff," whispered Ginger, reaching for her hand and squeezing it.

She lay, stupefied by liquor and exhaustion, feeling as if the space between their beds was a chasm. Taffy had caressed Jefferson's hand furtively as she'd showed them her room. She'd pointedly told Jefferson, while Ginger was in the bathroom, "I *could* have stayed with Jody tonight."

Now she lay on her back, wearing only her white slacks, sleep nowhere in view, and reached down to the floor for the last crock of wine. Ginger slept, as always, deeply, peacefully. The peace wine had brought—where had it gone? Where was her golden day? She couldn't stand to lie alone, awake, empty-handed all night. Should she wake Ginger? No. She'd worn her out with her impulsive adventure and should let her rest.

She could visit Taffy. Just to talk. It would fill the long hours. She reached for another drink. They said people who drank alone were alcoholics.

"*I'm only home in your hands,*" Ginger had said, trusting all that talent, all that beauty, all that ambition and grace to her.

She opened her eyes wide. Was she having nightmares? Why all these troubling thoughts? A chill crept through her like the sudden night earlier on the porch. She stared into the dark horrified at the thin line between staying in bed and leaving Ginger's side; between talking to Taffy and—

Once again, she reached for the bottle, felt its round solidity in her grasping hand, drank. The wine trickled down between her breasts. She sat up, drank again. Ginger didn't stir.

She rose, heart thudding with excitement and fear. Trembling, she pulled the white v-neck over her head, picked up the bottle, and crept out to the hall. Taffy's door was ajar, open on yet another promise.

DUTCH AND SYBIL I:
ELEANOR ROOSEVELT'S GARDEN

Dutch and Sybil passed in the hallway of the senior citizen apartment building many times before they ever really noticed each other. The first time they met, after beginning dance lessons in the same class, they stopped to talk.

For a sixty-eight-year-old woman, Sybil was still terribly shy. She was shortish, but not spread out, and her hair was a grey-streaked brown. Her glasses reflected the electric light of the hallway as she looked up toward Dutch. "My husband hated to dance," she was saying.

"So did mine!" Dutch was tall and gangly. Her body was quite youthful looking, but her face showed its sixty-seven years in lines and saggings. Her short crisp hair was a fading reddish-brown that would go white practically all at once whether it happened this year or in twenty years.

Sybil went on, "I decided I wouldn't look a bit more foolish than any other old lady in the class."

Dutch had to lean forward a little to catch Sybil's soft words. "You're not so old!" she said, throwing her arms out wide.

It seemed possible to Sybil that she hadn't noticed Dutch before, the way she bounded down the hall. Except for the plastic flowered shopping bag, from the back she might have been a teenaged boy.

In the elevator Dutch was smiling, pleased to be getting to know Sybil.

Both women had moved in only a few months before, after the deaths of their husbands. And neither had been ready to make friends until recently. Now Dutch was determined to have lots of friends and had been planning how to throw herself into the project, in the same way she threw herself into everything.

They danced again later in the week, or tried to. All the ladies seemed to believe age had robbed them of agility, rhythm, energy. Except for Dutch, who really worked up a sweat until she had the basic four-step right. Then she set out to teach it to Sybil. At the end of the hour, they were the stars of the class, and everyone applauded their skill.

"Let's go to Doggie's to celebrate," Dutch suggested.

Once a year Sybil dutifully went out to dinner—on Mother's Day, with her overbearing, kindhearted children. But this invitation excited her. Out on her own with a friend! She was a woman of the world at last!

That Saturday night they sat in Doggie's cocktail lounge drinking old fashioneds. Dutch was still excited from her triumph in dance class. She asked endless questions about everything—including her new friend. "Tell me about yourself," she said. "Where are you from?"

"Right here." Sybil's eyes were sparkling.

"All your life? Me too! I grew up on Poplar Street and settled with George over on Glade, in that nice little apartment complex."

"Poplar!" Now Sybil was excited too. "I was born and bred two streets over. . . ."

It seemed they had lived parallel lives within the same town all those years.

"Though come to think of it," Dutch said when the second drinks came, "you do look like someone I should know, just a bit."

"We could have been friends if I hadn't gone to sister school."

Suddenly they had too much to tell each other. All through the salads, the fried seafood platters, the key lime pie, they reminisced about their adjacent lives. Even in the hallway outside their apartments it was hard to part. But Sybil said no to a nightcap. All that food and excitement had made her positively lightheaded! She needed badly to lie down.

Through the rest of the winter they kept up their lessons, getting the steps down better than anyone else in the class. Now and then, at exhibitions held for all the classes, they would have to dance with one of the old men; but it was always disappointing, pushing a clumsy, well-meaning soul around the floor while pretending to follow him—when they themselves danced so well together they could really put on a show!

One night they sat in the third floor lounge watching the last snowfall of winter settle deeper and deeper over the beach. Tomorrow they would bundle up and push through it with their high boots till they got to the water's edge where they would watch the sea take chunks of the cold white stuff away.

But tonight it was nice, sitting like they were. Though Sybil admired her friend's energy, the way she high-stepped through dance classes and her life, she wore her out so. Dutch appreciated Sybil most at these times too, when her little friend's hands flew at their needlework and she talked and talked long after the others had gone to bed, sharing more and more of herself with Dutch.

"You know what I've always wondered about you?" asked Sybil.

"What, little dear?" Dutch had come to call her friend that.

"How in the world you got your nickname."

"That's easy! When we were kids, George and I were awful poor. But by the time we started seeing each other we both worked. I couldn't let him pay my way everywhere, it went against all my common sense. When he finally gave in and agreed to share costs he started teasing me about being his dutch treat. After a while it just got to be Dutch. And I liked it much better than Annabelle."

"Oh, goodness, yes."

In front of the big snow-filled window they smiled at each other over the pink and blue afghan Sybil was making for an imminent grandchild.

"I'm getting tired of dutch treats," Sybil said with a sigh. She noticed Dutch's hand go quickly to her heart. "What's wrong?" Living where they did, it was impossible not to worry about heart attacks.

"Nothing." But Dutch's face didn't look like nothing. She finally asked, "Do you mean you're tired of *me?*"

"Oh, no!" laughed Sybil. "Not at all. Why I've never been so not-tired-of-anybody before in my life!" She blushed scarlet.

Dutch sighed in relief.

"All I meant," continued Sybil when they'd both calmed down, "was that I'd like to cook you dinner sometime. We always go out and I like that, but as long as my little hole-in-the-wall is home I'd like to have you as a guest in it."

Dutch hesitated. "I could never ask you back because I'm such an awful cook. Once George hit me with the saucepan I'd burned the peas in." She pulled her sleeve back to reveal a burn scar.

Sybil looked torn between laughing and crying. "Tell me," she asked, leaning forward, "aren't you sometimes just a little bit glad—" and she lowered her voice to a whisper "—to be free?"

Dutch's eyes cleared and the life in them spilled over onto everything. Sybil, looking radiant, tenderly returned Dutch's gaze. They reached for each other's trembling hands and held, all four hands resting atop the unfinished afghan on Sybil's knees.

Then they pulled themselves back. Sybil took up her needles.

Dutch said, "I'd be delighted."

It was so late when they went off to bed that not even the insomniacs were creeping around the halls. They kissed each other's cheeks and parted, a little puzzled over all they felt.

Spring came and their friendship grew deeper, their dancing feet fleeter.

"Oh, the smells of the flowers! I don't think they were ever so sweet before," breathed Sybil. While the others on the senior bus tour to Hyde Park explored the Roosevelt mansion, Sybil and Dutch stayed in Eleanor's garden.

"I heard about her last year," said Dutch. "About her and that woman reporter."

"What about them?"

"How they *were* together." Dutch seemed to search for words. "You know."

"Not like *that*. . . ."

Dutch nodded. Sitting very close on a stone bench, they

looked away from one another. Soon they got up to walk above the river and chatted of their grandchildren, about whom they seldom spoke. Yet all the way home on the bus Sybil's head lay on Dutch's shoulder, and each pretended to the other she was asleep.

Dance classes were over. But summer band concerts were being held Friday nights on the town green. Dutch and Sybil both confessed to having longed to go for years. But somehow, with their husbands uninterested, then ill, neither had ever gotten there. Now summer rushed on toward them and with it the excitement of dancing out of doors. For it was mostly senior ladies who went to these concerts—and the rule among them was, anything goes!

They practiced and practiced in the empty recreation room, enjoying this time they could dance together. One day as they rested they defiantly said that they would indulge themselves on the green. Even though everyone would be there, they would dance together.

"To heck with them all," said little Sybil.

"Why shouldn't we if we'd rather?" Dutch challenged no one in particular. "So the men don't feel left out? I gave *years* to taking care of men. So no one is shocked? We're too darned *old* to start worrying about shocking people now. Next thing you know we'll be dead and there'll be no dancing then!"

Sybil shuddered visibly at the thought and watched as Dutch paced away her anger.

"Besides," continued Dutch, "all the men *are* old. We're still spring chickens!"

Sybil heartily agreed and put aside the bed-jacket—disguised as a gift for her daughter-in-law—that she was secretly knitting for Dutch.

They went off to the center of town to buy ball gowns. Or so they called them. In reality they chose pastel-colored pantsuits. Sybil bought powder pink with an orchid jersey.

Dutch bought the exact same style, but in white—"like John Travolta"—and a lavender jersey.

The Friday night before the band concert Sybil and Dutch were both restless. They decided to walk on the beach till dark—at least they'd get out of their apartments. It was a warm night, a little muggy, and the sand was easy to walk on from an earlier rain.

"There goes Belle," said Dutch, pointing to a figure swimming laps between the breakwaters.

"Do you think we'll be in that good shape when we're eighty-two?" asked Sybil. As was her habit, she had taken Dutch's arm.

"If we keep our spirits in as good shape as hers."

"What a scrapper she is!"

"She got that new handicap ramp put in the recreation hall."

"And started the Walking Club."

Dutch stopped. "We'll follow her lead, little dear. I want to live a long time now."

Sybil had that tender look in her eyes again. "Do you think we'll still be friends at eighty-two?"

"Oh, yes," Dutch said quickly. She looked as if she might take Sybil in her arms, but instead turned toward the horizon. "How beautiful the setting sun is."

Sybil sighed. "All those colors. Like Eleanor Roosevelt's garden. I wonder—was she happy with her friend?" They hadn't mentioned her since the senior tour.

"They say so," Dutch replied quietly.

It was so natural, later, for Dutch to stay the night.

"We'll have peach brandy by the fire," Sybil giggled.

Dutch was watching her friend's preparations. "The fire?" she asked.

"My poor worn out television set. Why don't you look in the guide? Maybe we'll find an old favorite on the late show."

The convertible love seat was all made up for Dutch to sleep on. It looked so cozy they climbed in together to watch *Dracula* and drink their peach brandy.

The set flung light at them; the room was filled with flashing shades of grey. As the mournful background music rose and fell, the ladies snuggled closer and closer, holding hands, looking at each other, they eyes wide with fright, their lips wide with smiles. Now and then, one watched the other's face a while, as the TV light hid, revealed, softened the aging skin.

One such time Dutch lifted a finger and ran it across a line on her friend's face. Sybil didn't stir, but her chest rose as she breathed her response. It grew warmer and warmer in the room, but they wouldn't kick the covers off, afraid to break the intimate spell.

The horror show ended and Sybil rose, reluctantly it seemed, to turn it off. She paused before the TV. It was time to go to her bed.

"Come lie with me awhile," said Dutch.

"Oh," Sybil said in a tiny voice.

For a moment all the two women could hear in the dark room was each other's breathing. A plane passed overhead then and, as if to move under cover of its sound, Sybil scurried to the bed and thrust herself against Dutch's waiting body.

This time they both breathed "Oh" as they pressed against one another and let their lips touch once, twice, then for a long, long time.

For an hour before the first concert, people could be seen all over town walking slowly toward the green, or loading lawn chairs into back seats of cars. Dutch and Sybil hitched a ride with Bella in her old van.

"Got your partners lined up for dancing yet, girls?"

Smilng shyly at Sybil, Dutch answered, "No problem there."

As she parked, Bella surveyed them with a keen eye. She smiled and said, "Save one for me, won't you?"

Twilight was still a way off, but the sunlight was softer then it had been all day. It lit up the greens of the grasses and leaves while the breeze set them all dancing. People were settling around the bandstand, the band was setting up, there was a flurry of activity to match the flurries of excitement in Dutch and Sybil's stomachs.

Of course the mayor had to puff himself up and make a speech, but as soon as he shut up, the bandleader whipped out his baton and began a lively Dixieland number. Dutch and Sybil blended right in with the applauding crowd, their greying heads nodding, their feet tapping with the rest.

It wasn't until the third number, when the bandleader paused to urge the audience onto a wooden platform, that the dancing began. Tiny Bella was up there first, her fused hip making her dance look elfin as she limped and swayed and clapped her hands and shouted to all the others to join her.

Then it was Dutch and Sybil who drew the eyes of the crowd. Around the platform, dance after dance, the lady in powder pink followed perfectly the lady in white. When everyone danced in a line, as at dancing class, it was high-stepping Dutch who found the rhythm, who smiled and laughed and drew even more dancers up. Sybil was right beside her, now and then helping the less adept.

How elastic Dutch and Sybil's bodies seemed, how filled with life their eyes and smiles. Their faces were flushed with a youthfulness not found in the faces of the teenage boys who lurked in shadows, jeering at the dancing ladies. Dutch was handsome, agile, debonaire. Sybil was lovely, graceful, gracious. Their high spirits, their obvious *happiness* spread like lingering sunshine way after dusk set in.

The park lights went on. A few dancers tarried in a fox trot, then a goodnight waltz. There was a summertime of dancing on the green ahead of them.

Bella, tired for once, had left and taken the lawn chairs. Dutch and Sybil strolled toward home. Their jubilance had peaked long ago, and they were tired too. But Sybil never expected to see tears falling onto Dutch's new white suit, brilliant under the streetlamps. "What is it?" she asked.

Dutch couldn't talk yet, could only walk, and cry. But finally they reached a lightless spot where hedges hid them from view of the houses, and no cars passed.

Dutch stopped. "All those years," she was saying.

It was Sybil's turn to strain to hear her now.

"All those years with . . ." and Dutch's voice broke. She had to pull herself together all over again. "I suppose it was worth it to bring the children into the world at least. . . ."

Sybil watched her tall and slender lover in the dark, filled with pain to see her pain, filled with pain herself as she anticipated what Dutch was about to say.

"All those years with *husbands.*"

The street was utterly silent. The horror of Dutch's realization was too heavy for them. They swayed there beside the hedges, facing each other, hands linked.

Dutch's voice came one last time, the voice of someone in torment: *"All that wasted time."*

MARIE-CHRISTINE I:
VALENTINE'S DAY

The sun, reddish from smog, set later and later in these waning days of winter, like a blazing heart reluctant to rest. It was Valentine's Day and Marie-Christine longed more and more poignantly for the last moments to pass before she could lock the vibrator shop and step into daylight. This particular night she longed too for someone with whom she could share the last few hours of Valentine's Day.

She'd broken up with her most recent lover and hadn't the heart, yet, for a new full-fledged relationship. But Valentine's Day was meant to be shared and the frequency of her sexual fantasies was getting out of hand.

She finished the display cases and straightened, pushing

back her loosely curled hair. *"Merde!* I will *not* spend Valentine's Day alone," she vowed in her French-Swiss accent. Tonight, somewhere, somehow, she would find .a woman warm enough, appreciative enough, romantic enough—and free enough—to celebrate with.

The shop door opened. Annoyed, Marie-Christine set the duster on its shelf. But she was smiling when she turned. She was, after all, a working girl, and she'd just have to wait till after hours to begin her hunt. Smoothing her soft mauve sweater over loose but clinging slacks, she took a closer look at her customer.

"May I help you?" she asked, her voice melodious, reassuring in this shop whose wares frightened many of its first-time customers.

The woman, in white uniform shirt and pants under an open black trench coat, was shorter than herself; her hair, also short, was wavy, black mixed with iron-grey. Laugh lines sprang into the corners of her eyes as she looked up. Then she sniffed the air audibly, nostrils flaring. "Tabu?" she asked, her lips half-smiling, teasing.

"My favorite scent," replied Marie-Christine. Instinctively she emphasized her accent. Was she beginning her hunt so soon?

"Mine too." The woman's hoarse laugh shook her lean frame. "Never *wear* the stuff," she added, the laugh lines deepening, a twinkle appearing in her eyes.

Mid-forties, thought Marie-Christine. She liked her lightly-lined face, the soft wide lips, her humor. A rush of excitement spread from her cheeks to her chest, to her fingertips, to her thighs. "Our newest model . . ." she said, indicating a vibrator on the glass case between them.

"So that's what they look like." Gingerly, the woman took the vibrator from Marie-Christine and examined it as if it might bite her. She looked up, the laughter in her eyes a cover now for embarrassment. "You think I'm pretty naive, an old dame like me."

"Not at all. Most of my customers are even more terri-fied than you."

Again, the hoarse, body-shaking laugh, but hollow, Marie-Christine noted, as if an automatic reflex. "So it shows, does it?" the woman asked.

Marie-Christine just smiled, keeping eye contact till the woman looked away. A pleasant chill swept down her back.

"Would you believe—" She was a native New Yorker from her accent—"my doctor sent me?"

"Dr. Sterne?"

"Not the first referral she's made?"

"She's an—ah—old friend."

The teasing half-smile returned along with a nod of understanding. The woman spoke quickly, nervously, as if energy ran loose through her body and into her words.

"Bursitis," she said. "I'm a baker. Heavy trays, bowls. When you're twenty-five your shoulders don't notice. After forty-five. . . ." She shrugged, then winced and massaged her right shoulder.

Marie-Christine found herself, against all her own business-hour rules, wanting to touch that salt-and-pepper hair. She laughed to herself. It would be just like Sara Sterne to assume a patient was having trouble making love—either to a lover or to herself—because of shoulder pain, and prescribe the vibrator for the shoulder, knowing very well that the patient would find it useful in other ways too. But then, perhaps Marie-Christine herself could help. She had a quick vision of the baker making love—all that ex-perience—Marie-Christine was only twenty-nine.

"You can try it out back here," she said slowly, almost seductively. She pushed a heavy blue curtain aside to reveal two doors beyond.

"What's this?" asked the woman, laughing that empty laugh, vibrator in one hand. Then her tense face loosened promisingly. "If I choose the left hand door I get the girl? The right—I'm stuck with a boy?"

Marie-Christine hadn't been certain before that the woman was gay. She smiled, looking her up and down slowly to let her know about herself. She wondered if the baker was warm enough, appreciative enough, romantic enough; then decided that with this one she'd settle for free enough.

The baker still hesitated. "Seriously," she said, edging inside the left-hand room, the vibrator held before her, a skeptical look on her face. "Is this the one you'd recommend?"

"It's got every optional attachment imaginable."

"Yeah, but do I need them all?"

Marie-Christine returned to the showcase, slipped another out. "This is my personal favorite," she said, running a hand along its shank, as if just her gentle touch could turn it on. "But then," she said, looking at the floor as if to make her point, "I don't use it for bursitis."

"Oh?" asked the baker. "What do you use it—" She stopped herself.

Marie-Christine looked up, caught the baker blushing.

The woman laughed again. "That's okay, that's okay. Sorry I asked." She put down the first vibrator and reached for the second.

"It's quite wonderful," offered Marie-Christine.

"I'm sure." The baker blushed even more, smiled an embarrassed smile and pulled the door shut behind her.

Back on the sales floor, Marie-Christine listened for the low buzzing sound. Her heart was fluttering. Out the windows the city's lights beckoned against a charcoal sky, one cluster after another, promising and promising.

The left hand door opened. "Uhh—" said the baker before laughing that tight embarrassed laugh. "You just rub with it?"

Really, thought Marie-Christine, it was perfectly simple—unless you *wanted* help. Was this a good sign? She went to the door and in a moment set the vibrator buzzing and massaging the woman's shoulder.

"Ohh . . ." the baker said.

"Good?" To relax her further, Marie-Christine asked, "What else have you tried?"

There was a silence, as if the baker was considering what she might mean. "Shots. Heat. Not using my arm," she finally answered.

Marie-Christine worked on.

"But how could I stay out of work? I've got a co-op, three cats, a mother to support."

"You live with your mother?" She wasn't interested in *that* type.

"No. I give her money." She twisted her head to see Marie-Christine. "The bakery was my father's before he died."

Marie-Christine thought of her own mother, wife of a diplomat, presiding over banquets—and over any scandals Marie-Christine might precipitate. They sent *her* money to stay in America.

She laid her free hand on the baker's uninjured shoulder. She could feel both shoulders give up their tension and the warmth of relaxation suffuse them. A smell of hot bread seemed to come from the baker's body. When her breathing slowed Marie-Christine guided the baker's own hand to the vibrator, silently taught her to use it, her plum nail polish bright against the baker's hand so pale it looked as if the years of white flour had stained it. She stood behind her, massaging the back of her neck hard, gently, hard again, struggling with herself toward and away from this attraction, so unlike anything she'd allowed herself in the shop before. But she smelled the bread smell in the baker's hair, felt the warmth of her rising more, filling the whole tiny room. Her own nipples belied her better judgment, and rose longingly, as if reaching for the warmth beneath this well-worn white shirt.

She was startled when the baker said, a smile in her deep quiet voice, "I'll take it!"

Marie-Christine moved away, relieved the spell had been broken. The baker turned to look at her. One brow was arched, the wide mouth smiled a crooked smile.

"And how," asked Marie-Christine as professionally as she could with a voice that had dropped to a husky level, "do you want to pay for it?"

They were facing each other, both grinning widely.

"That depends."

It was Marie-Christine's turn to arch a brow.

"On whether I'll need cash to take you to dinner tonight."

Marie-Christine took the vibrator, caressing its tip as she did so. "Mastercard?" she asked. "Or Visa?"

* * * * *

"I'd rather just call you Baker," she said at dinner, running one stockinged foot up Baker's leg under her slacks. Baker had turned out to be charming, the owner of one of the best bakeries in the city, and full of funny stories about fussy customers.

"Okay," Baker agreed and they went on to a bar, to dance to romantic waltzes. Marie-Christine could tell, just by the way Baker held her elbow as they crossed the streets, what kind of dancer she would be. And when they danced there was a certain way that Baker led, deft and clear, gentle and so aware of Marie-Christine's body that she could tell what sort of lover Baker would be. Her body felt *heard*.

As they spun their brief romance under the dance floor's twirling lights, Marie-Christine celebrated her find. Baker had this night off, but worked six others, her schedule opposite from Marie-Christine's—a relationship was impossible. She pressed against Baker's soft shirt, wishing it were summer so that she could be wearing less and could feel Baker and Baker's hands against her bare skin. They danced more and more closely; Marie-Christine had a special affection for Baker's thigh and the sensations it produced between her legs.

But it hadn't been an easy thing, getting Baker to come home with her. The closer they got to Marie-Christine's apartment, the more Baker lost the warmth that had flowed bit by bit into her laugh over the evening.

Now they sat together on Marie-Christine's Salvation Army couch and its soft black crushed-velvet throw. Marie-Christine asked Baker to light every candle in the room, and excused herself to change into a flowing, clinging green gown.

When Marie-Christine returned, Baker was turned away from her, staring toward a candle flame. Baker cleared her throat abruptly. Would she explain her discomfort?

"I'm not sure I should be here, you know," she said. "I mean, I want to be with you, Marie-Christine, you're a breath of fresh air in my life, but maybe I don't want to be with you for the purpose you might expect." Only her laughter was nervous now; her body looked too tense to move.

Marie-Christine sighed deeply, breathed again, took another sip of brandy and savored its rich flavor. Perhaps Baker was too good to be true. The nervousness, the worrying—what was bothering her? She said nothing to Baker, only ran her long fingers across the crushed velvet. She could smell the fresh Tabu she'd applied. If she remained patient she'd soon be touching that greying hair, and unbuttoning the slightly soiled white uniform shirt. She licked her lips as she imagined it loose, hanging open over the baker's unconfined breasts.

Baker was speaking again. "I fell in love with a woman

for the first time at nineteen. We stayed together eighteen years." Baker paused, and stared downward, her brow creased. The brandy glass went round and round and round in her hands. After a moment she looked at Marie-Christine again. "It was terribly painful. I haven't had another lover since."

Incredulous, Marie-Christine asked, "You haven't had a lover for *nine years?*"

Baker shook her head, looking at the worn oriental rug as if ashamed of herself.

"And you don't even own a vibrator?"

Baker took a breath and let it all out in her hoarse full laugh.

"Did I say something wrong?" inquired Marie-Christine, playing with Baker's hair.

In answer, Baker pushed playfully against her hand. She looked as if she certainly liked being touched.

Marie-Christine settled further into the couch, enjoying the way her gown enveloped her yet let her feel her own nakedness beneath it. She set her glass down, its liquid amber tilting from side to side. Then she took Baker's glass from her and placed it beside her own. "My heart is bruised too," she said, her fingers trembling as she began to unbutton Baker's white shirt, "and will be gentle with yours." Baker's skin felt like silk under her fingers, smelled richly of her famous bread. As the shirt fell open, though, a sweeter smell emerged, as if only a pinch of sugar, a pinch of cinnamon, had been used for flavoring, yet permeated everything.

Baker watched Marie-Christine, her forehead again creasing with wrinkles. "I just don't know if it's worth it," she uttered, her voice breaking, a flush of desire spreading over her face.

"This?" Marie-Christine asked. She finished with the buttons, drew the shirt out of Baker's pants and slipped her fingers underneath.

"What if I fall in love with you?" Baker asked shakily.
"That would be wonderful!"

Baker looked at her with worry—no, fear—in her eyes.
"But . . ." she said.

"Tonight. I'd love you to fall in love with me for tonight.
Only tonight," she finished in a whisper, close to Baker's ear.

That she'd have her heart back intact after Valentine's
Day was all the reassurance Baker seemed to need. The words
had barely left her dry mouth when Baker's hands reached up
and firmly closed around her arms.

"Baker," she said, as if tasting the name. Her voice felt
like butter. So did Baker's lips on Marie-Christine's throat,
her cheeks, her lips. Her tongue tasted like the sweet rolls
served with dinner. Her hands were smooth and dry as if,
indeed, she had dipped them in flour first before pushing
Marie-Christine's gown up to her thighs.

God, she wanted this woman. What incredible hands,
square but quick, short-nailed and everywhere on her now
that she'd let them loose. "Let's go to bed," she said just as
Baker began to lift the gown toward her hips. It was all she
could do to keep her thighs together when they felt as if
they were melting apart.

Baker opened her eyes; they filled with panic. At the
sight of Marie-Christine she whispered, "I'm not sure I'm
ready for this." She replaced the gown over Marie-Christine's
legs as if to spare her modesty.

Marie-Christine sat straighter. "Baker, my Valentine,
you've been ready since long before you stepped into my
shop."

Baker nodded. "I know, I know. But I never want to
feel that bad again."

She slid a gentle hand up along the outside of Baker's
loose white slacks, from knee to crotch. "Let's bake up the
sweetest memory we can imagine tonight. Decorate it with
fancy hearts and bunches of flowers. If it's sweet enough,

it'll eclipse your old bad memory which you must be very very tired of, *n'est ce pas?*"

Baker, in another of her sudden turn-arounds, laughed with real gusto. "You," she said, following as Marie-Christine rose, "you make it sound so possible."

Very slowly and deliberately Marie-Christine blew out all the candles but one, and carried that one as she led Baker by the hand toward the bedroom.

At the bed she touched more intimately than before the coarse waved hair. She removed Baker's shirt entirely. Her breasts were soft dough. She kneaded them. Baker's nipples had hardened; she shivered as if cold. Marie-Christine feared she was losing her again, but Baker's laugh was completely warm this time, sincere. Her breasts moved with it.

"My heart," said Baker, holding out a hand curved as if around some small precious object. "I trust it to you tonight."

"Thank you," she whispered, looking into Baker's eyes as she unbuttoned the white pants. She closed her own eyes then, lifting the gown over her head. When she opened them Baker was pulling her own white panties off. "Gingerbread girl," she whispered to Baker. "Under white frosting. Oh, how sweet," Marie-Christine said, licking and licking.

When their naked bodies met under the covers it was shock that did, this time, melt her thighs apart, that let those quick pale fingers find her drenched labia. Baker was moaning and moaning.

She relished Baker's total concentration on her, feeling admired, respected, safe because of it. No wonder Baker had been devastated. Eighteen years of devoting herself like this to one woman? She pulled Baker to her, made her stop as she held her tight. Ran her hands down the back that felt more like a twenty-year-old's than a forty-six-year-old's.

Baker shuddered. "It's been so long," she said and began to move again. But her concentration wasn't so total and she lay back now and then, wonder in her eyes as Marie-Christine caressed her body with those fingers tipped in plum, or with her mouth, or with her full breasts.

And this was the recipe that worked, finally, this moving, resting, giving, taking, till they both came, separately, with all the urgency that had brought them together.

The red hearts of Valentine's Day, laced in white, danced in Marie-Christine's head. Each heart birthed another, and another, a swarm of them loosed and coursing through her veins, down her limbs.

"Happy Valentine's Day," she breathed then, as Baker's hand began to stir her once again.

BABE AND EVIE I:
SUNSHINE

Sun shone through the slats of the venetian blinds. Babe crossed the living room and ran her hands down their smooth surface, trying to shut the sun out more. But the lines of light only shifted slightly on the orange rug. There was no keeping all the heat out this summer. Any more than there was any keeping Evie in.

Babe sighed. There wasn't much she could do. After all these years together, if Evie had something to go through, she'd just wait it out. And keep her mind occupied as best she could. At least Evie hadn't moved out. As much as Babe loved this third-floor flat at the top of one steep staircase out back, two dark and polished dress-up flights through the front of the old house, she couldn't live there without Evie. Even if Evie had said she was only staying because she had nowhere else to go. Even if Evie had taken to sleeping on the couch.

She touched her newly permed and rinsed hair. She'd known Evie wouldn't notice and had done it for herself, partly from habit, partly from certainty she would feel better. She did.

And she was circling, she knew that, circling and circling. Fifty-eight years old. Another Saturday night coming on fast. All dressed up in a new hairdo with no place to go and no one to go with. Evie, just retired from thirty years on her city job, had virtually disappeared from her life when she should have had even more time for Babe. What did they use to tell one another, all misty-eyed with happiness at the kitchen table on a hot summer's afternoon like this, sweat running down the red and yellow flower decals on their pretty glass pitcher—we ain't got much, but we got plenty.

She could circle no longer. She crossed the room and this time ran her fingers lovingly over the organ keyboard. It had been sitting there, the little electric organ, since Christmas. She'd longed for one for years and years. She walked over to the old flowered couch and sat gracelessly, as if her legs had lost the will to hold her up, as if she'd finally let go of the will she'd clung tightly to these two hard, hard months. At the office, where she'd asked for extra work to keep herself typing at the other keyboard in her life. Grocery shopping, agonizing over quantities of Evie's favorite foods, because she didn't know if she'd come home for dinner. In bed at night, turning to slip an arm across the absent Evie, burrowing closer and closer to no one.

The organ, sedate, solid, stared back at her. She'd wanted it ever since she had to sell her piano when she left her parents' home to live with Evie. Before Evie got the City job that paid decently. They'd needed money to buy furniture—

like this couch they'd reupholstered twice since, each time in a brighter flowered pattern.

Christmas day she'd played the organ gingerly, reverently, afraid to smite the air with her unpracticed chords. It was too real, this making of music. Somehow she hadn't dared play as she longed to, really play like her heart was in it, play loud and lovely like the lovemaking she'd shared with Evie. Even at Christmas time, a month before Evie's retirement, she'd felt as if she had to walk on eggs. Evie flared at the slightest thing. Went silent for hours at a time.

And when Evie had left her job, Babe had played only when she was certain to be alone, and then as quietly, tentatively as she could—the way she felt. In the house Evie was so moody, and would putter in the spare room she'd converted to an electrical shop years ago, but not putter seriously, like she'd planned. Evie had been going to rent a storefront up on the Avenue cheap, from her brother's boss's friend. But she hadn't done any of it. Who knew when Evie would be home now, darn her. Who knew what she'd do now, Babe thought a little desperately, throwing up her hands, but at the same time rising, going to the organ, switching it on.

She played a chord. Delicious, she thought as she felt its vibration like a shiver down her back in this small hot room, glowing with indomitable sunlight and color. She played the same chord, louder, then louder still, and as she began to play melodies it was the colors she sought, even in the simplest strains of old songs—in "Side by Side," in "You Are My Sunshine," in "Sunny Side of the Street."

How they'd sung, over the years, rowing up at the lake on Fourth of July picnics with Evie's family. Riding with a busload of City employees and their families to a boat tour around Manhattan. Or walking, just walking the neighborhood at twilight and quietly singing together, letting their love rise on sweet melodies into the air, into the world that wouldn't accept or acknowledge that love, but let it live.

She paused for a moment, heard a step, then another, on those funny back steep steps so typical of their flat, so typically, oddly like them, different yet exactly right for what and for who they were. Of course it was Evie, come home to putter, to stare at the TV, to ignore her. Well darn it, she'd got her hair fixed for herself and she was going to play for herself, the heck with old sourpuss Evie.

And she played. Some of the familiar songs, some new ones in the song book that had come with the organ, by the Beatles and by Elton John. In her mind she had them stomping, all the world out there, dancing and clapping to her beat, swaying to this rhythm of love, of feeling, of daring to enjoy no matter what her fears.

A breeze pushed the venetian blind in. She could see a corner of that long iron handrail and realized that Evie had stayed outside the door. She craned to see. There she was, sitting out there all this time, listening. What was she thinking? Was she just waiting till Babe was done, till everything was over so she could steal inside and be at peace?

She played on a little while, a favorite old sad song called "Melancholy Baby." Then she stopped. She'd had her hour. The sun was slipping in some other direction now, and the room had darkened.

Into the silence came the sound of applause, strong and loud on those back stairs. Evie had opened the door and stood there grinning shyly in a way Babe hadn't seen in so long, and clapping up a storm.

"I didn't know you were *that* good," Evie said.

Babe tried not to smile too hard, but knew her face had gone all bright with flowers of pleasure and embarrassment.

Evie stepped into the dimness, her hands still. She just looked at Babe, then slipped her hands into her pockets, and shuffled off to the kitchen.

Babe held her breath. She stood, her back to the organ, eyes fastened to the flowers on the couch, hoping without words. Just hoping.

"Hey Babe," she heard Evie call from the kitchen. She heard, too, the sound of ice cubes swirling in circles against glass, that old summer sound of happy afternoons. And she heard whistling. Evie was whistling "You Are My Sunshine," slowly, as if pulling it back into the light of day was painful.

By the time she reached the kitchen she knew what she'd see and there Evie stood, stirring ice into fresh-made lemonade, in the old glass pitcher with red and yellow flowers.

"I was thinking about going out for a pizza tonight," Evie was saying. "It's kind of hot to cook. You want to go out for pizza with me?" She motioned Babe to the table. "Have some lemonade," she said, sitting in her chair.

Slowly, Babe walked to her own chair. It was the kitchen the sun had shifted to, and the sun lit its colors till they glowed bright as the living room had.

"Thank you," she said as Evie handed her a glass of lemonade, ice cubes crackling in the heat. She was trying to talk to Evie without letting her voice sound as misty as her eyes had gotten. But all she could see was a picture in her mind of the two of them, glowing like their kitchen, singing all the way down their funny back stairs on their way to dinner. She couldn't wait.

JEFFERSON II:
IN AND OUT OF THE DARKNESS

Ginger ran up the stairs from the subway eager to reach the wide bright Grand Concourse. She breathed deeply. Somehow today the long subterranean ride up to the Bronx, her training ground, had seemed like a dance in an underworld inferno—perhaps the inferno of her own mind which seethed with conflict.

"Yo, *Gin*ger," sang Aisha, the heavy fifteen-year-old in Ginger's class who moved like thick slow cream, like lava just starting to pour. Ginger smiled broadly at this devoted student who, each week, just happened to be passing her subway stop.

Aisha cradled her oversized radio on a hip and bent into

45

the rhythm of its song, fingers snapping. This was their tradition. Ginger leaned toward her, her own fingers snapping. They moved, the tall, copper-haired white woman and the big-boned, brown-skinned adolescent, into a rhythmic gait that would carry them all the way to class at the Neighborhood House. Ginger loved being with someone who saw the world as she did, through her ever-moving body.

"You're going to take this job, right?" Aisha asked, popping her gum in emphasis.

Don't show it, don't let the kid know, she told herself as she teetered again on the brink of plunging back into the inferno of conflicts she'd fought in the dark tunnels of the subway. Safely balanced for the moment on this familiar Bronx street, she laughed aloud.

"You laughing at me, Red?" asked Aisha in a hurt voice.

She shook her head. "No, at me," she answered. "Me and all the dank nasty tunnels in myself that this job offer— and an old friend showing up on my doorstep—made me see."

At least she could laugh at the dark places in herself that compelled her to try and take care of Aisha, of everyone, everyone and anyone who came along. If she was going to teach full time at the Neighborhood House she'd have to learn not to take each aspiring dancer under her wing or she'd burn out. And now, on top of that decision, her old lover Jefferson was asking for one more chance. If she wanted to give Jefferson that chance, she'd better learn fast.

Aisha was waiting for an explanation. But how could she tell her about Jefferson's hand last night, reaching to take hers, as Jefferson explained that she'd gone to AA for help, had given herself over to anything that would lead her back from the drunk to the living—and that it was working.

How hard it had been to let that hand go, that beloved hand with the same bleached quality to it as Jefferson's graying hair, as if both had been well-used in the world. She could see that hand, feel it again, a sensitive capable hand she remembered people frequently offered to shake, as if for the strength of it, as if to see how a hand should feel. She remembered, too, its warmth on her when they'd last been together, remembered the feel of it and felt it again, its warmth coursing like some intoxicant through her body.

Aisha was looking at her strangely, but seemed to take comfort in their matching steps. The girl lived with an aunt's large family, her mom gone off, her dad a dancer who skipped into and out of her life just enough to give Aisha a taste of home to long for. And to give dance a taste like home.

"*Boy*friend trouble again," said Aisha with a sneer and a loud gum snap.

"Kind of," she answered. She'd let Aisha assume her ups and downs had been with men. It had been six years since she'd been with Jefferson, six years she'd been trying and trying again to settle for someone other than Jefferson. Searching for someone who looked as handsome in her soft corduroys and a cracked and faded brown leather jacket. Someone else who lived, loved, understood life with her body. Someone who knew why Ginger danced the rumba as she washed the dishes, who glided with her when she was happy, saw the slouch of her body when she was down, who understood being loved with arms and legs and breasts as well as with a heart.

"You *will*, won't you?" urged Aisha.

Just Jefferson's words last night. "You *will*, won't you? Think about trying it again with me?" She had to remind herself what it was Aisha was talking about. "You really want me to come teach up here full time, don't you?"

The radio song ended and an announcer came on with rapid-fire words.

"Uh-huh," said Aisha and popped her gum.

They reached a cross street; Ginger stopped at the curb's

edge, her whole body tensed at the sound of a siren, her muscles feeling like a hundred brakes on all her moving parts. The ambulance passed, racing in the direction of the walk-up where she'd been raised by her pert, pretend-nothing's-wrong mom, and her beloved, now-you-see-him-now-you-don't dad. "I can remember," she said as Aisha crossed the street with her, "leaving this behind to get famous, to set the world on fire."

To move, she thought, up and out of her dark tunnels by going to college. To escape the dim battleground of her parents' apartment and take that fiery glory she'd inherited from her dad out into the world away from his alcohol. A world where she found herself trembling and scared till Jefferson came with a glory of her own and confidence enough for both of them.

She had drunk in that confidence like a liquor, to fill the place inside herself that remained afraid, the belief that she needed another's strength to lean on. It had taken her many years to learn—and even then she learned only through her arms which had held this reeling, weeping, vomiting lover, that Jefferson's confidence had been as swollen with liquor as had Ginger's dad's.

A new song started. The Bronx street was full of radios like this one, playing warring tunes. Once she'd danced in a production of *West Side Story;* now she wondered if today's rival gangs claimed their own musical turf. She and Aisha walked to the new rhythm. "And you," she told the girl, "you want me to come back here, to the place I had to leave."

Aisha shifted the radio to her shoulder. "You set all the fires you going to *down*town, Red. Now you need to pass that torch."

Her mind shut down, a siren of its own screaming No! No! No! But her honest body nodded its head in agreement so that Aisha, seeing this apparent assent, began to grin.

"No," Ginger said quietly to the blunt cruel wisdom of a fifteen-year-old evaluating a forty-year-old.

Aisha's face fell. She shrugged and opened the door to the Neighborhood House, taking the stairs to the second floor two at a time. Ginger paused, looking up the long steep climb. It was true that performing careers were for the young—or the very hardy.

She'd had her turn in the limelight. "They're waiting for you out there," Jefferson used to say whenever she needed to hear it. "Waiting for my leaping redhead. Thee isn't a thing in the world that can stop us, baby!" Last night the handsome face had been drawn with sadness, had finally been humble. Wanting Jefferson, Ginger's arms had yearned to open. And it wasn't just her arms that remembered the long nights together, remembered the dancer and the athlete, their legs entwined, breathing hot words into one another's mouth. It had been all she could do to make her body keep its silence.

"You coming?" called Aisha.

Now she sought within that dancer's body the energy to climb a flight of stairs. Was this happening to convince her? Was her body insisting that performing was behind her as well? No one hired forty-year-olds. She knew that, yet kept on, using her reputation, her connections, her ripened talents and experience.

This flight of stairs—if only she felt like flying as she often did on stage—loomed higher than she could imagine she could pull her body, weary with conflict. The relative languor of teaching was seductive. Were her rhythms shifting? Her body had not stopped dancing, though, in every move that she made. Nor had it stopped wanting the hands of Jefferson. Still, she feared a misstep, she needed to be certain this dance was her own.

The full-length mirror doubled each girl and each bright-colored leotard. She unbelted her trench coat, unwrapped her long skirt and stood before the bending, kicking, stretching images. Slippers, sneakers, stockinged feet, slid or thumped on the polished wood floor. A faint scent of sweat, of hot young perfumes, reached her.

"Three, four, five, six!" she cried in a challenge to establish the rhythm of the room. Surely this was one of her great pleasures, this weekly trip home. It was more than just an act of giving, it was a reminder of how much she'd accomplished.

A little one approached her. "My cousin, she lives in Florida, she wants to know would you autograph this for her?"

It was a programme from a performance she'd done with a traveling troupe. "Is she a dancer too?" she asked, signing with a flourish.

The student nodded shyly and ran, self-consciously graceful, to lay her prize with her coat.

"One, two, shoulder up; point, *kick*, step, *kick!*"

To think she'd once depended on Jefferson's "Of course you can!" assurances to even get herself to classes. Had waited out her infidelities, worried after her drunken car crashes, suffered through her hungover irritability—just to keep Jefferson's love, to keep the one sure means she had to shore up her self-confidence.

The sunlight seemed even brighter across the flashing leotards. "Three, four. Lead with the *hip*, follow *through!*"

They were reviewing a dance choreographed by one of the older girls. It was Aisha's turn this week to teach her own dance and Ginger went to her where she rehearsed by herself. "What did the scale say this week?" she asked.

Aisha turned and looked fiercely into her eyes, corn rows seeming to bristle, fingers never seeming to cease their beat, which was out of sync with the music that played. Ginger worried about her. The truth of the dance profession was that slenderness succeeded.

Aisha spoke. "The scale? It said, Red's got *nothing* to worry about. It said you, Aisha, are gonna be the world's first full-figure dancer. They'll be *begging* for more once they see my style."

Ginger sighed, watching as Aisha performed a difficult combination. The girl *was* heavy. Her addiction was to food. "You may be right, Aisha," she told her. The girl turned back toward the mirror, snapping, snapping. "You've got the creativity, you have all kinds of drive. Who knows? Dance has come alive to innovations before."

Teaching—was this to become another unlit seething pit of misdirected energy? Once, with her own constant uncertainties, with Jefferson's demand for mothering, with their draining scenes, she'd thought Jefferson her fatal addiction. She'd resented Jefferson for interfering with her career, for keeping her from the very top of her profession; yet she'd been convinced that only she, with her sacrifices, could make Jefferson happy.

Now she knew her addiction had been to focusing on anyone but herself, to giving all of her attention to others' needs. To holding herself back by setting obstacles in her own path. How it had obscured her own artistic fears, over and over, when Jefferson had withdrawn into moody hung-over silences and Ginger, feeling the familiar pangs of abandonment, could ignore everything but this crisis with Jefferson.

It's so much easier, she wanted to tell Aisha, to drug yourself with liquors, with lovers, with food, than to take that final step and free-fall alone to success or failure.

Instead she said, "Looking good," and went to dance with the others. She let herself enjoy this simple piece of choreography, enjoy the girls and their intent rush to go even as far as she had—and she'd gone far despite the dragging of her own brakes as she clung to her security. Maybe today she would enjoy Jefferson in the same way—if she kept in mind that a lover was a woman and a home, not a fix.

"Dance World!" she cried as the music ended. The girls ran to her and sat at her feet, expectant. They weren't exposed to much dancing up here, just as she hadn't been, growing up. "I saw Bebe Miller's Company do three pieces at the Dance Theater Workshop last week. One was called 'Trapped in Queens!' "

"*Queens,*" jeered one girl.

"I'll say they're trapped!" said another.

They all laughed. When the chatter died down Ginger said, "I thought that title might inspire one of you."

"You mean, like, 'Trapped in The Bronx?' "

Excited, she described the piece. If she accepted this job she could take them to performances. But the thought of spending the rest of her life watching gave her a hollow, dead feeling. Couldn't she keep dancing, but less, and only where she wanted to, if Jefferson moved back in and shared expenses? Wouldn't her exhaustion ease when her conflict was resolved? When she had a home, and arms, to rest in? Out of the corner of her eye she noticed Aisha fidgeting.

"I thought you didn't get nervous," she teased.

"This dance is real important," Aisha answered. She was no longer snapping her gum.

"How come?" asked one of the others.

Aisha, sitting with her legs outstretched, leaned over them to reach to her toes. " 'Cause how else we going to convince Red to stay here with us unless we're worth it?"

Ginger shook her head and smiled. Did Aisha have a drinking family too, that she drew the whole world onto her shoulders? She reminded herself that the girl's success did not depend on her teacher alone.

The girls were silent, as if waiting for Ginger's decision.

The room seemed to grow dim. Had someone pulled the

shades? Had the sun gone in? She felt swept under once more by the swirl of her confusion. She couldn't face giving up dance; her body was shutting down against the pain, starting with her sight. She leaned into, away from, over the precipice of the unknown. Before, she'd never been able to balance her two passions: dance and Jefferson. One had always drained the other. All these little girls, what had she to give them from her failures?

She pulled back her hair, refastening it in a leather barrette. She willed her vision to clear. "It's not," she explained, "what you're worth to me. But what *I'm* worth."

Aisha looked puzzled.

"She means she wants to do what's best for *her*—am I right? asked an older girl.

She just smiled in reply, and signaled Aisha to prepare for her dance. *Was* the girl right?

Dressed in tatters, Aisha moved in her liquid way, like hot lava slowly pouring from behind the screen that served as a curtain. In each hand she carried a shopping bag filled with more tattered clothing. A homeless woman: the sight struck Ginger's heart. Hadn't she been feeling just that— homeless? Performing, she was out there all the time, exposed to the public. Since she'd given up Jefferson she'd never even wanted to be home.

Aisha had selected a gospel song, slow and sad to start with. But as the beat picked up Aisha's dance grew livelier. The bag lady was busy, perhaps seeking out a nest—a home on the edge of her own volcano.

Each time Aisha set down her bags Ginger wanted her to stay, felt the yearning to nest in her own body as well. And each time the woman lifted her bags Ginger grieved, and saw more clearly that a chance for Jefferson was a chance for herself.

The beat strengthened and Ginger began to clap, to tap her feet, to sway with the music and the homeless soul Aisha had created. The girls around her joined in as if they'd been holding their dancing hands and feet in check. Aisha moved with her back straighter, her bags lifted higher, as if, nearing home, she had wanted to show that her burdens felt lighter. Ginger felt the tension of the piece and her thighs tightened with pleasure, as if Jefferson's hands were on her.

Sitting cross-legged on the shining floor, she knew this was not the place to recall the magic of her nights with Jefferson again, but the passion of the piece took her back to how she'd loved to be inside Jefferson. Two, sometimes three fingers plunging to Jefferson's gasps as those strong thighs quivered, then tensed, as her hands let go their grip to convulse against Ginger's back.

Soon now, she thought as Aisha's growing smile signaled the resolution of the piece, soon she'd descend once more to the subway, to the inside of her volcano, carrying as if in two bags of her own the two fiery passions of her life. Could she balance, finally, Jefferson and dance, as she rode past lit stations, through tunnels, into and out of the darkness?

She'd been watching Aisha break her patterns, erupt in molten energy that sought the light, that claimed dance as a home for herself. Jefferson had broken her pattern by getting sober. Could she break her own by facing the dark side of herself? She'd learned she was strong enough to live without Jefferson, but was she strong enough to live with her, to take care of herself instead of trying, vainly, to fix Jefferson?

Aisha set down her bags, pulled from them rags for a bed and a clock she wound till it loudly, dissonantly, ticked a new rhythm into her formless life. Ginger watched her nesting movements and was stirred in every cell by dance as expression, by the very thought of moving the world with motion. She envied this gifted student her performance even as she learned from her.

She watched intently, the life in her limbs flowing, flowing, sounding in the explosions of her clapping hands. Couldn't she, couldn't she with all she knew now build a home solidly of love? And teach through dance this life she was just learning? To stop performing now and limit to a classroom what she had to teach would be for her a free fall to failure, not success.

The class was standing and she'd risen too. They were all clapping, stomping, eager to learn this dance of joy Aisha was just ending—or just beginning. The girl twirled around the rag bed, empty bags flying, her smile as strong as the sunbeams that shone like spotlights around her.

FROM A NOVEL IN PROGRESS:*
DUSTY EATS OUT

"Dusty, lover?" Elly asked. "Aren't you *ever* going to go down on me?"

It was a hot, moist, blue summer dusk. They'd been putting in sixteen hour days at the diner since they'd bought it two months before. At the end of this infrequent day off they'd begun making love early. Noisily bedding birds were a love song outside their window.

Dusty pulled her big-boned naked body away from the smaller Elly and stared anxiously through the smoky light

---

*Dusty and Elly are also characters in the author's novel *Toothpick House.*

at her. Without glasses, the last of Elly's makeup seemed like smudged dusk. "You mean . . ." she faltered, unable to say the words she needed.

Elly twisted close again and smoothed back Dusty's short, wavy auburn hair, tonguing an earlobe. "I mean with your mouth," she whispered, rubbing a sharp hip across Dusty's belly. "You know, like this," and she sucked on the earlobe, then flicked it back and forth with her tongue.

"I never did that before."

Elly stopped. Her younger body, small-breasted, with fragile-looking slender shoulders, glowed in the dim light, sweaty from humidity. The shock on her face began slowly to fade to her slow, teasing smile.

Dusty dove, belly down, under a pillow. Partly to escape that knowing smile. Mostly to hide her humiliation. They'd been together several months now, she'd been making love with women ever since she'd entered the Navy twenty-two years before, just out of high school.

"How could you *never* do that?" Elly asked in astonishment. "Though I can understand not wanting to with old prune-face Rita."

In the seventeen years she'd been with Rita, Dusty had only tried it once, after an old Navy buddy had brought home some postcards from Denmark. She'd slid down Rita's body, getting as far as rubbing her lips across her pubic hair. Rita had stopped her. "I guess," she said to Elly, her head still under the pillow, "it just never came up."

Elly hung over Dusty's broad back so that her breasts just grazed it, and said, "Do me, lover?"

It seemed to be Elly's favorite phrase, said with her Tennessee drawl exaggerated, a sure-fire way to turn Dusty on. But did she want to do it?

"Don't you want to?" Elly asked, her breasts tracing double patterns on Dusty's back.

She shrugged, half-hoping Elly would give up and drop

the subject. The room was growing darker. Outside there was a lull in the birds' chatter and she could hear the ducks quack across the little pond that had come with her older, tiny house.

But Elly just stretched against her so that her slightly long brown hair tickled Dusty's neck. Again Elly whispered into her ear. "Then let me do you."

"Elly . . ." Dusty complained, her tone half-aggrieved, half-pleased and excited.

Elly began to tickle her, giggling. "Don't you hide your face from me all night, you old bear. You come out here and get yours."

Dusty twitched and held her breath to defend herself from Elly, but the woman was unrelenting. So she heaved herself up and pushed Elly back downward on the bed. "I can't," she said, breathless. There was nothing like a few hours alone with Elly to make her forget her role in the world as a competent, hard-working cook and restaurant owner, to bring out the awkward kid in her.

"Why not?" asked Elly, apparently perfectly happy to lie beneath her and grind her pelvis upward instead of down. Their hot damp bodies made a sucking sound each time Elly broke contact. "Here," she said, gripping Dusty by the buttocks, urging her forward with her hands. "Scoot up over my mouth."

"El!"

Elly laughed at her shock. "Why not?"

"I didn't even have time for a shower today!"

Minutes later, Elly was perched on the closed toilet seat as Dusty showered.

"You sure are taking your sweet time," Elly said when she'd finished removing her nail polish. "Y'know, lover, if we don't take more time off from the diner my nails are going to look like I do them with your rose clipper."

Dusty turned off the water and dried every available inch

of herself, twice. She even passed a hand between her legs and smelled her fingers.

Elly was laughing as she followed her back to bed in the dark. A car started on their suburban street. "Be home by midnight!" called a mother, her voice shrill. Elly pulled the curtains shut. "You're so dry now I could start a fire with you, lover," Elly said, passing a hand over her skin.

Dusty narrowed her eyes, a secret half-smile on her sensuous face.

But Elly had become dead serious. She switched on a bedside light and slowly, deliberately untied Dusty's white terry robe. "Yeah," Elly said, her voice deep, slow, "and that's exactly what I'm planning to do."

In the heat Dusty lay still, robe spread open, long fleshy legs gently urged apart, her lover's mouth breathing hotly on her skin still warm from the shower. "Can't we turn the light off?" she asked.

Elly had parted her outer lips and was blowing between them. She looked up. "But you're so pretty to look at!" Her laugh, sometimes, was like glass wind-chimes.

"Pretty?" She squirmed as Elly studied her.

Laughing, Elly said firmly, "Pretty. Even butches are pretty down there."

"You could at least close your eyes." She paused, relishing a favorite fantasy of hers. "And put your heels back on."

"Why, Dusty," Elly said in surprise, but said no more. She quickly bent to the floor and slipped into her black patent leather high heels, giving Dusty time to admire their effect on her little feet and long shaved shapely legs. Then she nestled between Dusty's legs once more and her tongue licked, flat and hard, the length of Dusty's inner lips.

She gasped at Elly's touch. Nothing had ever felt like that.

"You like it, lover?" Elly asked, talking into her, starting a new rush of feeling.

She no longer minded the light being on. The sight of Elly's delicate fingers holding her apart, of her tongue touching her *there*, of her soft moisture-smeared lips pursed above her—it was as if some bright hot star shone on them, illuminating Elly for her further pleasure.

Elly pulled her inside her mouth. All of her. And Dusty felt the flood of her excitement immerse the tongue that entered her. Then the flood spilled out and out till her thighs were wet, the bed was damp, till she came against Elly's warm soft tongue.

Elly lifted her shining, smiling face and moved up beside her in the bed, kissing her all wet like that. "You've got the sweetest smell," she told Dusty. "And you taste like—"

"Sex," Dusty finished happily. Surely the glow she felt showed. She propped herself on one elbow and looked at Elly. "You smell like the bed after we've been doing it for hours."

Elly kissed her wetly again. "No, lover. I smell like *you*. This is what *you* smell like." Leaning back, Elly asked, "Want a cigarette?"

"No." She was wondering what Elly smelled like. "El," she began, thickly, clearing her throat, but the words were still too hard. Gently, she pushed Elly back onto the bed. It was Elly's turn to grin. Slowly, she moved where she could begin to kiss Elly, as if her mouth was merely meandering over her moist skin, as if she had no particular purpose in mind.

But by the time she'd kissed all inside her thighs, Elly's breathing had changed. "Lover," she was saying, the drawl coming from deep in her throat.

Dusty breathed deeply, through her nose. The smell of sex was everywhere. It was intoxicating. She floated on it, in it, wishing she'd had the privacy in the service to explore like this, the self-assurance to have tried again with Rita. She was resting her head on Elly's thigh, breathing her in.

"Lover, lover . . ." Elly repeated, twisting toward her.

The high hot flush of her contentment fled. Give her a kitchen and she could perform culinary miracles. Give her a house, a diner, anything in disrepair, and she could fix it. But give her a girl, and some sex right now—what should she do next?

But Elly's hands pulled her head closer. All that curly hair tickled Dusty's nose. She pushed her tongue through it, found the parting of the lips, but was stuck there, couldn't get further.

Elly reached down and opened herself to Dusty's tongue.

The boldness of the act sent another rush through Dusty. Her tongue all at once knew its way. Elly moved beneath her, already awash in a sea of her own making, her hands in Dusty's hair, twisting, curling, grasping, then falling limply to the bed as she groaned—no, cried loudly in a way Dusty had never heard a woman cry out before.

Elly pulled her up, her eyes barely open, her mouth faintly, contentedly, smiling, "You *sure* you never did that before?"

Dusty wrapped her sturdy arms around Elly, pressed her lover's head against her broad shoulder. The hot night trapped their fragrant heat around them, and they lay content in the glow of it. Darkness had fallen completely and with it silence. A breeze pushed past the light curtains. Dusty let her eyes close.

Some time later, Elly switched the light off. One small bird cried out in the night. Dusty, half-dreaming, wondered if stars ever fell through bedroom windows. How the white glare would glow, turning dark to dawn, waking the birds to sing their love song once more.

DUTCH AND SYBIL II:
BEACHFRONT HOTEL

"Why not?" asked Dutch.

They were sitting on the lawn outside the senior citizen housing project. It was only early summer, but the heat was overwhelming.

"I'd just as soon sit right here under a tree and catch the breezes off the water," Sybil answered. "Why get into a stew packing and rushing off someplace no better?"

Dutch fanned herself with the travel brochure. "For the adventure of it! We're not even seventy yet. Look how many years we have left—why spend them all under this old tree?"

"I love you, dear Dutch," Sybil said softly, "but you're

not always very wise. I'm perfectly agreeable to a winter trip somewhere warm."

"So am I. But why can't we have two trips?"

Sybil looked very small, very frail as she turned her hands helplessly palm side up and shrugged. "The expense," she said.

"Damn the expense!" Dutch said vehemently, then looked around her. "Pardon my French, but there isn't enough to make a difference in our children's lives when we pass the money on. They seem to eat the stuff whole! Let's use it now. Do you realize it's been a year for us? This would be our anniversary trip!"

They smiled fondly at one another, then shook their heads as if in wonder that they should, at their age, after all their years of marriage to men, have become lovers at all. Finally, Sybil blushed. She often told Dutch how *inappropriate* it felt, their passion in old age.

But a week later they were all packed for their anniversary trip.

They sat in their new apartment drinking a toast of peach brandy. "I don't think life has ever been so wonderful," said Dutch, who would talk nonstop as long as Sybil would listen about their luck in finding one another. "Our own private apartment together without any old *ladies* peering at us every time we touch. And I think you have such marvelous taste."

Dutch's studio had been a clashing hodgepodge of all her favorite things. In this larger place, even with all of their belongings, Sybil had managed to arrange everything so that it was either stored or displayed in harmony with everything else. What didn't fit—so long as it didn't deprive either woman of a past pleasure—was discarded. Both had found, with their new love, that they needed to keep a lot less of their pasts around.

"Have I told you how much I adore you recently?"

Sybil set down her crocheting. "Not since before dinner," she said, smiling.

Dutch moved next to her on the bench. "This will be our honeymoon trip." She slid an arm around Sybil's shoulders, bending to kiss her neck. "Ouch," she said.

Sybil turned quickly. "You mustn't bend that way!"

"Damned arthritis won't even let me kiss my girlfriend."

"Yes it will. You just have to let me help and not be trying to do everything yourself." She fit herself into Dutch's arms.

"I'd rather do all of it myself," Dutch crooned into Sybil's grey-streaked brown hair, her fingers tracing a wrinkle on her neck.

"You're impossible! Do you think you're a twenty-year-old boy?"

"Only if that would please you." She'd managed to slip Sybil's robe and nightgown from one shoulder.

"Heavens, no. I *had* one of those when I first married." Sybil leaned back while Dutch caressed a breast. "Besides, you do it much better than he ever did. . . ."

* * * * *

The ride up to northern New England was long, the bus noisy and the air conditioning inadequate. Stella from the apartment next door insisted on talking across the aisle to them. She'd tried to sit *with* one of them, complaining that Dutch and Sybil were too much together.

"Look how lovely!" said Dutch as they drove past the beach.

Sybil nodded tiredly. She wanted to rest, to enjoy the view tomorrow.

"Do look," Dutch insisted.

For her sake, Sybil craned to see out the window, then laid her head back. It ached, and Stella's chattering didn't help.

"Happy honeymoon," whispered Dutch as romantically as she could, with Stella leaning toward them.

Sybil's wan smile worried her. When the bus stopped she hovered over her and helped her down the steps. "Breathe some of this cool ocean air," she ordered, "and lean on me."

"You'd think you two were man and wife," Stella commented crisply behind them, "the way you take care of each other." One or two of the other ladies tittered.

"Need help with the young lady?" asked a blustery man who went on every trip, it was rumored, because no one could stand him back home.

Dutch straightened. She'd had about enough too. "No. We're fine," she snapped.

The hotel was striking: set on a hill overlooking the water, it was an old-fashioned, all-white structure with a porch running its full length. In the purple twilight its glowing white took on a certain majesty, as if it were meant for royalty.

Sybil stopped a moment. "This is the sort of place you dream about."

"Good dreams, I hope," Dutch replied. "Just a little longer, then you're going straight to bed. I'll bring up some food."

"No. I want to see the dining room, to enjoy every minute as long as we're here."

"Doctor Dutch's orders, Miss Sybil. To bed with you."

Sybil frowned, but was too tired, really, to insist.

Later, when there was a knock at the door, Sybil was already in her nightie. "Oh, dear," she said in alarm, reaching for a robe.

"It's only dinner," explained Dutch proudly.

As Sybil watched, astonished, a uniformed waiter wheeled in a cartful of silver-topped dishes.

Dutch stood rubbing her hands together in excitement. "Smells heavenly, every bit of it. And the wine is nicely chilled!" She tipped the man and looked toward Sybil. "What do you think? Can you eat a little snack?"

There was color in Sybil's cheeks now, and she smiled in pleasure even as she said, "You're a terrible spendthrift, Dutch Kurzawski."

"And you deserve a fine feast for your anniversary dinner in your honeymoon suite, Sybil Trask." Dutch ceremoniously removed the silver cover to reveal a steaming lobster bisque. There was also shrimp cocktail, melon and cheese for dessert. . . .

The next morning they could eat only a light breakfast. Sybil felt fit as a fiddle, she told Dutch, who nevertheless still hovered and led her.

They left the hotel behind them, blazing white, austere, and walked into a brilliant sunlight, the sky a vivid, cloudless blue. Along the water's edge they met Stella, Bella, and several other ladies, their shoes and stockings on the sand, their feet in water up to the ankles.

"Come on in," squealed Stella, "it's delightful!"

Bella was the only one in a bathing suit. "Delightful, my foot," she growled. "It's too cold to do anything but wade! Back home I can swim into the fall!"

Sybil and Dutch walked on. The little town sparkled as white as the hotel. Arcades stood next to hot dog stands, souvenir shops next to long, cool-looking soda fountains.

"I suppose we should have stayed on the beach with the ladies," said Sybil.

"Why?"

"I can almost hear them talking about us."

"If they have nothing better to do. . . ."

"But what if they finally see what's going on?"

One little shop featured jewelry. "We're careful," Dutch answered as she led Sybil inside. Then, examining a case of white-stoned rings, "How I'd like us to have matching rings."

"Oh, no."

"We could wear them when we're away from everyone else."

"If we had rings, I'd rather we use them. I'd love to see you on my finger."

"In more ways than one. . . ."

"Dutch!"

A saleslady appeared. "Not right now," Dutch told her. "Maybe before we go back home."

They wandered on. The town gave way to an amusement park.

"A haunted house!" Dutch said. "I used to love those."

"And a miniature golf course! I'd like to play before we leave."

In the park the wide old trees, ocean breezes rippling their leaves, tempered the sun's heat. Dutch and Sybil drew their sweaters tight across their chests. They crossed the parking lot to a small zoo.

"No worse than senior citizen housing," Dutch commiserated with a reindeer in a littered stall.

There was an artificial lagoon; boat rides were free. They chose a pedal boat.

"Careful, careful," warned Dutch.

Sybil said testily, "I can still walk."

At first Dutch ignored her mood. "How romantic!" she said as they moved slowly past the animals and under the trees. She took Sybil's hand, surreptitiously. "Is there something the matter, little dear?" she asked gently.

Sybil stopped pedaling; they began to drift toward the bank.

"You must keep pedaling or we'll go off course!" admonished Dutch.

"Stop for a minute then," Sybil said. "I don't want to pedal right now."

"What's wrong?"

But there in the shade, with gentle animals bleating, ducks quacking around them, whatever was wrong seemed less terrible. Sybil sighed and said, "I just needed a little rest. Can we stay out here forever?"

"Have you forgotten there's dancing in the hotel ballroom tonight? We need to get back soon and rest."

Sybil sighed again. "You're right, as usual. Let's stop in the little town and get fried clams for lunch. With tall glasses of iced tea. . . ."

"Sounds delicious, but maybe you shouldn't eat fried food after feeling so ill yesterday—"

"Lord, there's Stella and the whole crowd. Wave, Dutch, to keep the peace."

"I'd rather they kept *our* peace."

"It's a public park."

"Are they heading for the boats? Those doddering—"

"Dutch! Stella's no older than we are."

"She acts at least one hundred and two. Come on, let's go in."

Sybil let out a cry of disappointment. "I could stay on the boat all day!"

"With that crowd here we'll have to act like nice little old ladies. And don't forget the dancing tonight. We'll go find you a nice bland lunch."

"Yoo-hoo!" called Stella, pedalling furiously.

"We're just going in!" Dutch called back as sweetly as she could manage.

In their eagerness to see everything the crowd had apparently left Bella, slower than the rest of them, behind. Sybil and Dutch met her in the amusement park, swinging her fused hip as she walked, peering at the different rides.

"Been out canoeing, girls?" she inquired.

Dutch did not rankle at a question from Bella. "Pedalboating." She laughed. "I'm too old to canoe."

"I can, can-oe?" Bella chuckled at her own joke. Her lined face was tanned from swimming, right up to the line the bathing cap left. "That's nonsense anyway. I canoed with my husband just two years ago. It's very relaxing."

"You think we can do anything at all," Sybil said.

"You can bet your bottom dollar. The day I stop believing *that* is the day I go swimming and don't come back."

"Don't even think it."

"Some day, girls. Rather than be cooped up with a bunch of old hens I can't get away from."

"Isn't that just exactly what they are?" Dutch was glad of an ally.

"Say, the three of us ought to take a trip in my camper someday. I'd get to see the country like I did with my husband and," she winked, "I know enough to leave you two in peace."

Dutch and Sybil both flushed, but Bella said, "Let's plan something! It's just what we need." She swung off between two rides, calling, "Come back later, we'll ride the carousel together!"

They watched with affection, then looked at each other questioningly. Did Bella really understand?

* * * * *

It was how they'd fallen in love, dancing. Defying convention by dancing together, defying age by dancing at all. This was their first dance in a real ballroom, and they did not intend to miss it.

While the band took a break they went out on the long, elegant porch to rest in the cool twilight. Roomy wicker chairs with flowered cushions welcomed them. A waiter brought liqueurs.

"You're a heavenly dancer, dear one," sighed Sybil. "I

feel like a young girl in your arms. Or a cherished woman."
She blushed.

"And I feel like the self I never could be before we met.
Imagine, had we met back then, been brave enough back
then, what a life we would have led!"

"We would have traveled to Paris where there were
women like us."

"Paris, New York—we could have seen them all." With a
mixture of gallantry and caution lest someone see them,
Dutch leaned over Sybil's hand to kiss it.

"Hi!"

Dutch stiffened, pretending to examine Sybil's nail polish
in the fading light.

It was Stella, alone. She settled into another deep wicker
chair and fidgeted. "I saw you two enjoying yourselves, as
usual," Stella said, as if in criticism.

"We love to dance." Sybil's airy tone was forced, fell as
if leaden into the space between her chair and Stella's.

Dutch sat frowning into the twilight. Along the curving
shore, lights began to shine.

Stella continued to fidget. "I must talk to you both,"
she said in an uncomfortable, yet somehow excited voice.

"Is there something wrong?" asked Sybil softly.

Stella said, "I wouldn't bother mentioning this if the
other ladies hadn't begun to talk."

"Say it," challenged Dutch, her body gone cold with
fear.

At Dutch's words, the excitement left Stella's manner;
she seemed to collect herself before she went on. "There's
talk. About the two of you."

"What sort of talk?" growled Dutch.

Sybil's hand fluttered nervously at her throat, straightening her beads.

"Just that your . . . friendship may be more than it

should be. I'm sure," she said quickly, "that you know the dangers I mean. None of us want you to come to any harm."

Challengingly, Dutch asked, "How can a friendship be more —what did you say?—than it should be?"

Stella seemed to be searching for words. "You always want to be together," she said finally. "And then, all this *dancing*. It's not done. It's not dignified at our age. It's not *normal*."

There was silence on the nearly dark porch, except for crickets and the waves washing the shore before them. Dutch and Sybil looked at one another from their chairs, questioning, communicating with their eyes.

Without warning, as they reached across the space between their own chairs to clasp hands, the porch lights came on.

So it was in the kind, yet revealing, glow of the electric sconces on the walls behind them that they openly held hands for the first time.

Dutch asked Stella almost mischievously, "Are you afraid that we'll become lovers?"

Stella seemed at a loss for words. "Not exactly . . ." she replied. Her voice had become weaker.

They could hear Bella stumping across the porch toward them. Dutch smiled, waiting for her.

"Bella," Dutch said loudly and clearly. "I'm glad you're here. I was about to tell Stella not to worry anymore about Sybil and me. She says the ladies were afraid we'd become lovers!"

"NO!" said Bella, in comical mock horror. She slapped a knee with one hand, scratched her head with the other, and said, winking, "Whatever shall we do?"

Dutch laughed softly, squeezing Sybil's hand, looking at her once more. "You can relax, Stella—we already are."

Stella's hand flew to her mouth. "You couldn't—"

"I could and do love Sybil dearly and wish we'd been

lovers all our lives."

Sybil stirred, "I feel the same," she said in a voice weak with fear.

"Good for you," Bella said casually. "Come on, Stella, let's go dance." She laughed—apparently at Stella's discomfort at her invitation.

"What should I tell them?" Stella asked Bella, almost in a whisper. "The others?" She didn't look at Sybil or Dutch.

Dutch answered anyway. "Tell them what we said, of course," Dutch replied. "They're old enough to know about such things." She laughed aloud.

When Stella was out of earshot, Dutch leaned to Sybil. "Ouch," she said, cursing her arthritis again. "Are you all right?"

"Why did you *do* that?" Sybil moaned.

"I thought it would be best. What can they do to us? And you spoke too."

"Only so you wouldn't be alone."

"What was wrong with answering with the truth? Now we can buy rings before we go, stop hiding. It didn't bother Bella."

"You had no right," Sybil's tone was harsh. "It's my life too. I have to live with those ladies as well as you."

Dutch's tall body seemed to be wilting. "But I . . ." she began. They sat looking away from each other, staring toward the ocean in silence.

Finally Dutch asked, "Does this mean you don't want to . . . to . . . be mine anymore?"

For an interminal time there was no answer. Finally, Sybil said, "No. It doesn't mean that at all."

Dutch let out a long breath.

"You were right to say it, right to tell them. We haven't got enough time left to spend it all in hiding. No, that's not what's wrong at all. It's those ladies, and you."

"What do you mean? asked Dutch, leaning her angular

body toward her.

"I mean that I love you more than anything on earth, but sometimes, sometimes, you get a little too bossy with me, like my husband was—"

"I'm so sorry. I didn't realize. . . ."

"Let me say it all, while it's clear in my mind. *You* decided we should spend money on this trip. *You* decided we should make the trip at all. You almost bully me sometimes. I thought that's what you were doing just now, making up your own mind to tell them about us and the heck with what I thought or felt."

"Oh, no—"

"I see now that it wasn't it at all—we agreed to do it, somehow, silently. But I was mad at the same time about your bullying. And to top it all off, I was all tense and irritated from the ladies following us all the time, watching us, disapproving of the fun we have, the love we have. I was all tied up in knots about them and about you, and I almost, almost, let myself walk right off this porch in anger at you. But now I see it wasn't you at all, not tonight. It was everything all built up."

For a moment she stared out to sea. Then she leaned to Dutch and took both her hands. "I love you, dearest one. Do you think you can be less bossy? The way we can be ourselves together is what I relish as much as anything."

Dutch pulled away and began to wring her hands. She was crying. "I'm so sorry. I will change. I had to be like that with *him*. I didn't realize I was still doing it—and to you of all people. One reason I love you is for your independent spirit."

Sybil took back Dutch's hands. "Thank you," she said softly. "And the ladies, the web they were spinning around us with their suspicions, their fear of what we are—"

"It should go away now, Sybil. They can't do anything but accept us—or stay away from us."

"And you did that for us by telling them. It was so brave of you. And the chance you took that Bella really was on our side. . . . To think I was ready to give up on us because of their interference—"

"And my pushy ways."

"But I love how you know what you want, Dutch, and how you get it. I'd like to be more like you."

"I'll be more careful now, little dear." She took the handkerchief Sybil offered. "I won't step on your toes."

"Not even when we dance?"

As they grinned at each other they both realized the band had started up again.

"Are we going to disappoint all those old ladies in there? They want to see if we'll dare dance now!" Dutch said, laughing.

Sybil's eyes were shining with tears of gladness. "I feel like an ocean wave that builds and builds and builds—and then collapses, just happy to run back into the sea."

Dutch stood and bowed over Sybil. "Shall we go in?"

Sybil, rising, took her proffered hand. "I'd love to."

They walked, arm in arm, to the ballroom. Sybil smiled nervously up at Dutch. Everyone from the bus was there. Waiting.

Dutch swung Sybil into her arms and they began to dance. Graceful waltzes led to fox trots and polkas. Some of the women wouldn't look their way. Others smiled after a while, timidly, tentatively. The blustery man who went on every trip gaped, but his feet tapped out of control until he finally scooped up Bella to join in the dancing.

The four of them, then two more women, then another lady and man, danced the night away, till the band played "Goodnight Irene."

NIGHT 'N DAY

There was this dyke down at the Night 'n Day Convenience Store who was *so* in love, sometimes she couldn't even make change. Any good-looking woman who came in made Maggie think of *her,* and she'd go all soft inside, and look a lot less tough than she liked to think she did.

Maggie was tall, and broad-shouldered like her father. Though her skin was swarthy, her eyes flashed bright blue, especially when Heather came into the store. But she'd had acne right into her mid-twenties, and the scars still made her shy. Besides, Heather already had a friend, a tall, well-dressed woman named Irene.

"I love her, I love her, I love her," Maggie would breathe

over and over as she swished a mop back and forth across the floor.

"Hey, Maggie," the young boys who haunted the electronic games would taunt, seeing her stare into space at the cash register. Once she'd kept a tight rein on them, a carryover from her recent stint in the army, but now she was filled with a combination of lassitude and benevolence which allowed them to break all the rules. How, she would wonder, could she ever have thought all that rules stuff important? And she'd move up and down the aisles, straightening the shelves, breathing, "I love you, I love you. . . ."

One night Maggie got off the bus at work and thrilled to the sight of Heather and her lover driving into the Night 'n Day lot. She chanted I love yous as she crossed the street, arms swinging at her sides. She was euphoric when Irene pulled back out of the lot, leaving Heather in the store.

"Maggie," said the manager, "this is Heather, the new girl I told you I hired. I want you to train her to work on your shift."

Her heart began to thud as she looked quickly, shyly, at this pert, green-eyed woman, prettily dressed in a cowlnecked sweater and soft-looking rose-colored pants.

"It's getting busier in the store," he said, "and you won't be able to run things alone much longer."

The training took only a week, and it was only one more breathless, exquisitely suspenseful week until the first spark flew between them. They were working in the cooler, stocking milk shelves when their eyes met and then their hands and then they stared like they'd never seen each other before. The next night, in the back room, Heather dropped all the little penny candy bags and Maggie knelt before her to pick them up—and kissed her.

A little guilty at breaking up a three-year marriage, Maggie believed it was working so close to Heather that had started it, had pushed them out of control. Close to her at the register when it was busy, close and laughing together as they put the sloppy deli salads away for the night to the rhythm of "their" song on the radio. When they'd lock the door at twelve o'clock they'd be suddenly, irrevocably alone together as Maggie prepared the cash report and Heather fussed around her, straightening the counter, brushing against her, spilling the half-pound salad container of paper clips across her paperwork, so that they must pick up each clip, one by one. . . .

And then just as suddenly Irene would come for Heather. Irene would offer Maggie a ride politely, and Maggie would feel she must accept, or risk Irene's suspicions. She would watch the two of them in the front seat, *together* like that. Heather breezily telling tales of their customers: the crabby ones and the ones who made them laugh; Irene touching her so easily, so intimately, as if Heather belonged to her. Then they would pull up outside the house where she lived, and Maggie's soul would be wrenched right out of her to turn her back on Heather, to leave her to Irene and go into the little apartment she shared with her goldfish, where all she had was her store of the night's memories, and her dreams of the next night.

After that kiss in the backroom their passion gathered fast, and they found themselves plotting: when could they, how would they, how long would it be for. . . . Maggie would begin to tremble in her anxiety and eagerness. And they were lucky. Irene worked all day, while they didn't go in till 6:00 P.M.

At first all they dared were walks in the park where no one accompanied them except birds with songs of the spring. They'd find a wooded path far from the road and dawdle, Maggie entranced by the sheer pleasure of Heather's hand, its softness, its gentleness, its incredible sensuousness. What tongues each hand spoke! Maggie had held hands before, but never with such versatility, such perpetual motion, as if the hands were swimming, buoyed up by this sex-current that brought them together and together again. . . .

And when they'd stop, stop and turn to one another under the dappled sunlight falling through the ever-moving leaves, then there were Heather's eyes, so deep, so dark, so light, so blue, so green—always different. Maggie thought she could see clear down to her honest, loving soul.

Nor did Maggie stop her perpetual prayer. "I love you, I love you," she sang in her mind and sometimes now, quietly, aloud to the rhythm of their swinging hands. But when she wasn't saying it, singing it, she was talking to Heather, or Heather was talking to her, about their lives before, the future they were beginning to want together.

"I was so young," said Heather, twenty-three now. "When I left home I said I'd never go back to all the fighting and drinking. But I was so alone, so frightened. I hardly knew any other lesbians. Irene made me feel so *good*. And she seemed so dashing to me: she'd gone to college, had this important job. Yet she could fix the car, and cook. . . . I feel so bad, doing this to her, when she was so good to me most of the time."

"Most of the time? That's not enough."

"Oh, Maggie, you're right. It's not enough now that I know it can be different." Heather leaned into her so that they just brushed one another, each like a breath against the other's body, barely there, but a presence, a force unlike any that had filled the other's world before.

"And I had a *lot* of lovers in the service," Maggie confessed. "A month here, a week there. Once, a year and three months—and then she was transferred!" She shook her head. "I guess I was just killing time. Till you."

"But you're so experienced now," breathed Heather.

"In training, baby," Maggie replied, "getting ready to love you right." She tried to tell Heather with her eyes, how she'd love her right. How her hands would run over her naked body, over her and over her till her whole body floated the way their two hands did now.

And always there were the nights, at the store. Customers coming in would grin, buy twice as much as they intended, lean over the cash register to talk to Heather, to Maggie, to share the glow they saw, even if they didn't quite understand it. Sometimes the store was very busy, the two of them running different registers, back to back, bumping as they grabbed cigarettes, skipping around each other to the deli, the bakery cases. Late at night, during hours of moving together in a tight dance behind the counters, Maggie's heart just sang with the radio, the cash register.

One of those nights, her heart singing, Maggie couldn't stand it any longer. "Let's finish up quick, grab the quarter past bus, take it out to the city line where all the motels are. . . ."

Between customers, her cash drawer as wide open as her mouth, Heather looked at Maggie, frightened, saying, "Yes. Oh, yes."

Maggie shut down her register. They were at the bus stop by ten past, trying to blend with the shadows in case Irene was early.

The bus came, and they could see Irene pull into the lot as they pulled out.

"Poor Irene," whispered Heather.

"I'll take you back if you want."

"Never now. Never." They stared mournfully at each other. Heather looked trapped. "Well, maybe for a while. Maybe I'll have to go back just to explain. Just because—I *have* loved her, you know. . . ."

Painfully, Maggie sucked in her breath. Of *course* she'd loved her. There was no reason to feel hurt.

Someone on the bus opened a window. The cool night air came streaming back at them, like a splash of cold water. "Hey, this night's *ours*," Maggie said.

The haggard look left Heather's face and Maggie watched her sigh herself back into their world. The bus surged on, not making another stop until motel signs loomed before them like mirages in a desert and they got off.

"Did you ever do this before?"

Maggie had, in the army. But the motels around the base expected that. What if here, with no car, no luggage, the cops were called? She'd been this scared her first time too. But she strode confidently and said to Heather in her deepest voice, "We'll just go to the sleaziest-looking one we can find. They'll be glad of the business, and expect people like us."

People like us? she asked herself. Doing this together—what kind of people are we? Why don't we just come out and tell Irene? She looked quickly at Heather to see if she thought less of them for this night, but Heather was scrutinizing motels.

"That one, then," Heather said, pointing.

"Oh, baby, that's why I love you so."

Heather looked startled.

"Because you can just get right down to business like that. Just wait on a customer who's walked in on us, taken us by surprise. Or pick up all the little paper bags even after I kissed you. . . ."

"Yeah, but you do the kissing, you're the one who gets me so distracted customers can sneak up on us."

Immensely pleased with Heather's love, Maggie took heart and plunged into the red, white and blue office of the USA Motel. She hurried her way through the transaction, and went out into the night victorious, grinning, bearing the key.

Within moments they were, for the first time, fully inside each other's arms. "The USA?" laughed Heather.

"It's not bad," Maggie said, switching on the TV. "Oh, boy, a *Dirty Harry* movie," she said, pulling Heather down to sit on the bed by her.

"You like him?" asked Heather.

"Sure. Don't you?"

"All that violence. . . ."

"It's only a movie," Maggie reassured her, but sensed a greater fear. She turned off the TV. "Hey, I was just having fun. I don't have a TV at home."

Heather looked earnestly at her. "Maggie, did you ever hit a girl?"

"Hell no, baby. Girls are for loving, not hitting." Maggie held her, intensely aware of Heather's smaller body, her narrow, trusting shoulders. A fiery glow seemed to surround them and they reflected it with tiny pressures, sudden exhalations of breath. Each of Heather's movements, her sounds, inflamed Maggie, but still she held her, letting the glow grow brighter, letting its heat build, feeling the pressures last longer, the breaths become near-gasps, till she pulled back and faced Heather, looked at her, taking small, shallow breaths and shaking her head in wonder at the sight of Heather staring at her too, Heather's chest rising and falling as she struggled for breath too—

"Maggie, Maggie, Maggie," Heather finally said.

Was it a plea?

Maggie answered with kisses, a cascade of them up and down Heather's face and neck, within the V of her blouse, and back up, till she touched her lips with her own and guided her down, down, down on the well-used, but welcoming, motel bed.

"How I love you. Oh, how I love you," Heather said over and over that night. "You're *so* gentle."

"Girls should be," whispered Maggie, entering Heather again.

"I never knew, just never knew, how soft it could be," Heather breathed before she began to respond to Maggie's slow thrusts.

"Does she hurt you?" asked Maggie.

"Sometimes," Heather said a little later. "It's just like my dad. They both work in a man's world and have to be tough there. I said I'd never go back home, but living with Irene—I might as well have. When she gets like that, it's like she can't stop. I tell her and she tries, but something will go wrong at work and she gets rough with me again, like she's proving herself to me. On me."

"You mean doing this?" Maggie moved her fingers inside Heather.

"Ohh," moaned Heather. "Yes," she said finally. "And when she's mad, sometimes she hits me."

Maggie sat bolt upright. "She *hits* you?" But she could see Heather cringe at the suddenness of her movement and she lay down again, pulling Heather to her as lovingly as she could despite her own shock.

"She's always sorry afterwards. Swears she won't do it again. Makes it up to me. And I understand it's not really her doing it, it's all the pressure on her. She hasn't done it in a long time now, but—maybe it's wrong to think this—I keep thinking she might, she might."

"You sure can't go back now. Not after what we pulled tonight."

"Oh, I have to. It'll be okay. She's been fine."

Maggie began to argue, but remembered their night, the long hours ahead of them. Unable to imagine anyone hurting this precious woman, she gave herself up to the night.

* * * * *

The next day was warm, the breezes balmy, the birds restive with song. Maggie walked clear across town to pick Heather up. They'd agreed to splurge on a cab back to her place after collecting Heather's belongings.

The long, warm caresses of the night before were all that lingered in Maggie's mind. No, there were Heather's eyes as well, her breasts, her most intimate, delicate places. All the memories caused Maggie to smile at perfect strangers passing on the street. Middle-aged men tipped their hats to her in return; storekeepers sweeping sidewalks stopped and motioned her past as if she were a princess. Now and then a worry clouded her memories of the night, but she still felt as if everything were magic. Nothing bad could come out of such good and she imagined Heather was just fine, that Irene was calm and resigned. Why not? It was as likely as any other outcome, she assured herself at each twinge of anxiety. And Maggie herself would get adjusted to civilian life at last, get a better job, help Heather achieve her dream of going to the Community College. She began the day's chant of Heather's name and repeated it all of the last few blocks. She approached Heather's building singing aloud. But she grew suddenly silent at the sight of Heather crying on the front stoop. She rushed to her. "What happened?"

"She's up there," Heather said.

"Have you been out here all morning?"

"I went up to ask through the door if I could get my stuff."

"She isn't going to work?"

"Maybe we should come back another day. I tried to get you from a pay phone. I couldn't leave and let you go up there blind."

"She didn't hurt you?"

Heather, stiff from sitting on the cold concrete steps, rose and yawned tiredly. "I got out in time."

"I'll . . ." Maggie threatened, moving toward the entrance of the building.

Heather pulled her back. "No," she said wearily, laying a hand on Maggie's arm. "I've had enough fighting to last me a lifetime. Don't you be like that too."

"Like what?" Her hands were in fists; fury filled her muscles with a tension that sought release. "She's got no right to keep you out of your home. To try to hit you again."

"Maybe not. But I hurt her bad. I should have just faced her first, told her I'm too scared to stay with her. Told her how I feel about you, how meeting you made me see I didn't have to stay where I wasn't as happy as I could be." Heather's tone changed. Her voice caught. She looked up as if for reassurance. "I do think you're better for me. And Maggie, I love you so much."

Out on the street they could only touch with their eyes. But it was as if they could reach right into each other's souls. Maggie became aware of the birds singing again, remembered the sun was out, that Heather was coming home with her at last.

Unexpectedly, the heavy front door pushed open, slammed against the rail. The birds were startled into silence. Irene stood in the doorway, pain shadowing her face even in the sunlight, eyes rimmed in red, her hair in disarray. Instead of her usual well-cut, tailored clothes, she wore baggy green corduroys and a dirty sweatshirt. Her appearance was like a gust of cold wind and Maggie found herself stepping back. Heather stood her ground.

"Get your stuff out," Irene said in a dry weak cracking voice. "I don't want it around. I'll be back in three hours." She descended the steps shakily, holding the railing, and walked between Maggie and Heather, not looking at either, her hands, like Maggie's, in tight fists. Just beyond them she stopped and half-turned. "I'll be at the bar."

Heather moved closer to Maggie. "That means she's getting drunk."

"And that's when she hits you?"

Heather nodded yes. Hurriedly, she led the way inside.

"How could she, how *could* she ever hurt you?" Maggie demanded, more of the world at large than of Heather.

"I think because she grew up with it. In her house, like me."

"That's no excuse."

"No. But she says she can't convince her fists it's wrong."

They were packed and gone in an hour and a half.

For weeks after that they neither saw nor heard anything from Irene.

Maggie took Heather into her home and her life, taught her how to feed the goldfish. They started looking for a new place, big enough for both of them. But something had changed. It was as if Irene haunted them. Heather jumped every time a tall, well-dressed woman came into the store. Maggie kept talking about retribution, and began to feel mired in the Night 'n Day. Heather talked of being too dumb to go to college. Only when they were close in the dark, on their double mattress on the floor, when they held each other as tightly as they could, did the waves of the old overpowering feelings surge through them. But walking in the park, working in the store, it was as if that shadow of pain across Irene's face had been cast on them, too.

Soon the birds outside increased in number and the sun became brighter and more pervasive. Little by little their rhythm began to return at the store. The goldfish thrived, the new apartment was huge, its tall windows overlooking a tree full of birds.

One night they went out to the bar. A quick, covert survey convinced Maggie that Irene wasn't there. She held Heather's hand proudly as she introduced her to her friends. The flimsy wooden chairs, the too-small, formica-topped tables, the heavy smoke and noise, were all somehow comforting. For the first time they danced, they touched, they laughed together in front of others.

"Look Mag," said one of her oldest friends when Maggie went up to the bar. "I can see you're in love, but be careful."

"Of what?" asked Maggie, happily swigging beer from a long-necked bottle, her feet tapping to a song.

"I heard," her friend said, looking everywhere but at Maggie, "your girlfriend can be pretty tough to live with. Irene says when she starts telling you how to live your life the only way to get her off your back is to hit her."

She felt blood race to her head like a defending army. Her rage made her feel vindictive in a way she never had before. She said savagely, "Irene's just covering her own ass."

Back at their table she repeated the remarks to Heather and said, "I could kill her for bad-mouthing you."

Heather wouldn't tell her side to Maggie's friends, even to set the record straight. She was too ashamed to have stayed so long with a woman who hit her.

Their world, in the beginning so bright, so vibrant with their love, so welcoming and approving—a dance floor for them—had shrunk to a tiny shadowed space. Once more the only dancing they did, joyous as it was, was dancing in their bed. Lurking in the dark around them was their fear.

They shuttled back and forth between the Night 'n Day and their too large, echoingly empty apartment, their love grown circumscribed.

Then on a night they'd been called into the store because someone was sick, someone else fired, Irene walked in.

Maggie froze, just barely preventing herself from stepping protectively in front of Heather whose eyes were wide and staring.

But Irene looked small to Maggie, vulnerable. She was dressed once more in her natty clothes, with her hair combed exactly right, but she was thinner, and that pain-shadow seemed to have bled into her skin where it showed in half-circles under her eyes and in the deepening of lines on her face.

Maggie took her money for the cigarettes Irene bought, while Irene smiled weakly toward Heather, saying, "Look, I'm sorry," in a brave, but quivering voice. She was out of the store and back in her car before Maggie remembered her plans to kill her.

It was as if the whole world had exhaled in relief. Heather looked at Maggie, eyes bright as if with pride. Maggie knew, all of a sudden, that it was this confrontation they'd been waiting for and avoiding all at the same time.

"Thank you," said Heather. "Thank you," she repeated and repeated until her words were only a whisper.

Maggie caught her arms. "For what?" she asked, aware only that some huge weight had lifted from them.

"For not going over the counter after her, like you said you wanted to."

Maggie gaped at her.

"I was so scared. Scared if you hit her, you'd hit me—"

"No, Heather, I'd never—"

"—and if you hit me, that it meant I wanted to be hit." Heather spoke with the force of someone releasing something long withheld. "I chose you right after her."

"No," Maggie said. "I thought I was mad enough to, but I couldn't. In the army it was the same. I almost didn't make it past basic training. I was always too scared I'd hurt my partner."

Heather's smile grew wider. A certain light Maggie had missed came back into her eyes. For a moment she thought she heard the birds, but it was night. On the radio their song was playing, and when Maggie reached out and turned the volume up it was as if she'd turned their lives on again.

"Oh, Maggie," Heather said in a way Maggie hadn't heard in a long, long time. Heather had begun to sway to the rhythm of the song, turning to her chores looking as light as Maggie felt.

Together they put the sloppy deli salads away for the night, brought out new penny candy bags. Together they rang out the last customer, cleaned the store, locked the door, set out under a bright new moon to catch their bus home.

MARIE-CHRISTINE, II

Hints of warmth in the early spring air tantalized Marie-Christine. What she wanted was enough heat to raise a sweat, enough flowers to seduce her with scent, enough sun to flood her world with light.

She stood outside the Oscar Wilde Memorial Bookshop wishing for excitement and determined to find it. She could still almost taste winter in the air, but the shop's yellow light fell through a window as if to warm her tall figure.

Her frizzy blonde hair was encircled by a red silken scarf; gold earrings flashed every time she moved her head. Her body was lovingly wrapped in a mauve woollen cape, and her black baggy pants were stylishly tucked into high mahogany boots. She looked just the way she wanted to tonight: like a lesbian gypsy.

Inside the overheated bookstore she wandered restlessly from the dirty gay male cards to the lesbian books.

A light-haired butchy woman in a tweed cap stood studying a book called *A Woman's Touch*. Marie-Christine looked her over with frank boldness. She was neither too big for her taste, nor too small, and all the while she read she rocked, slightly swayed in her light-blue paint-stained coveralls and flight jacket. Marie-Christine liked her rhythm.

"Does it tickle?" asked Marie-Christine, looking at the furry collar of the woman's jacket.

The woman looked up. Her eyes matched the blue of her coveralls. "The book?" she asked, tilting it slightly toward Marie-Christine.

Ah-ha! said Marie-Christine to herself. *That* kind of humor.

"The collar," she replied in kind, running her hand across it, lightly, touching the woman's neck with her fingertips.

The woman didn't quite smile. Rather, she cocked her head, narrowed her eyes appraisingly, and dimpled one cheek.

Marie-Christine knew the signs of interest. Inside, she began to feel a fluttering. She did smile, stood back and nodded approval. "I'm looking for excitement," she offered, as if throwing one of her fuschia gloves to the floor.

The woman smiled back, removing her cap and extending a hand. "I'm not sure I've ever been called that. Mostly, I'm just Annie Heaphy."

"What," asked Marie-Christine, not releasing Annie's hand, "is it that you do for excitement?"

Annie shrugged—charmingly, thought Marie-Christine. "Schopenhauer at the moment," said Annie.

"New York offers no other distractions?"

"Getting a degree in philosophy is a hobby of mine,"

Annie Heaphy explained. "I've been at it several years now. It may take the rest of my life. I like to savor the philosophers."

"Could I interest you in savoring them while I watch? Or is it something you only do alone?"

The hint of shyness in Annie Heaphy's manner had not prepared Marie-Christine for her directness. "The Duchess first, or straight to my place?"

Still, it only took Marie-Christine a moment to respond, her tone taunting. "Are there philosophers at the Duchess?"

Annie dimpled the cheek, narrowed those eyes and turned from Marie-Christine to pay for *A Woman's Touch*.

As they walked toward the East Side she told Annie, "You're quite Irish."

"It seems I get more so as I get older. Till I was thirty I was a typical half-Scandinavian blonde."

They passed through the dark streets where tiny art shops separated warehouses. The sounds and fumes of cars grew distant.

"And you," said Annie, "you have an accent."

"I've kept it to make myself more intriguing."

Annie looked toward her from under the brim of her cap. She *seemed* intrigued as she measured Marie-Christine.

"French-speaking Swiss. My name is Marie-Christine. Father is a diplomat who agreed ten years ago to leave me in America if I'd just live my life quietly. Now and then he sends me a check to insure my staying. Or perhaps to assuage his guilt. This is lucky, since I can't even keep myself in wine, operating a vibrator store."

Annie, in a courtly way, held open an old, wood-framed leaded glass door and showed her into a narrow hallway. "My hole-in-the-wall," she said self-deprecatingly as they completed their four-flight climb. The apartment had been newly white-washed and still smelled faintly of paint. The trim was all in royal blue, rich against the bright white.

"What an amazing window!" It was tall, blue-framed, and somehow missed being filled with a view of other buildings. There were stars in the sky.

"I never have to pull that shade."

Marie-Christine turned from the view and watched Annie adjust the heat, then rinse red clear plastic glasses for wine. "So you drive a cab."

"About fifteen years now, in New Haven, and then here."

"New Haven? You were a Yale student?"

Annie shook her head.

With Annie's jacket off, Marie-Christine could see that the coveralls were open halfway down her chest. She enjoyed coveralls that unzipped to the crotch.

"Not me. I went with a Yale student though," Annie explained. "Five years. But when she finished her law degree she was west coast bound. Now we're bi-coastal lovers. I'm into dirty, ugly, crowded east coast cities myself, where the buildings block out the light and night is a bright as day."

They toasted, Marie-Christine from her perch on the still-warming radiator, framed by that blue window and the starlight. She was aware of the picture she made with her cape around her hips, her soft jersey clinging to her heavy breasts. "Schopenhauer," she prompted.

"You don't really want to hear all that."

"I wouldn't ask if I didn't."

Annie moved closer and studied Marie-Christine's face. "No. You wouldn't. But most women think I'm nuts to be studying philosophy."

"You may be the most attractive nut I've ever met then." Marie-Christine lightly touched Annie's cheek. She smiled in pleasure. "Tell me."

The change in Annie Heaphy was immediate. Her hands moved quickly through the air, her face became animated as she spoke. "Take art," she began, moving away from Marie-Christine to a table. "According to Schopenhauer, the artist creates certain archetypal 'ideas' that he calls—where is it now?" She ducked under the formica-topped table that obviously served as her desk as well as a dining place. "Here," she said, displaying a thick book. "The artist creates 'the permanent essential forms of the world and all its phenomena.'"

As Annie's hands shaped the air, Marie-Christine was stirred by her contagious excitement. She pulled the cape further away from her body and took several sips of wine. She could feel her face burning red.

"Artists," Annie went on, "don't see the way the rest of us do. They have a special vision, they reveal aspects of the world the rest of us—cab drivers and saleswomen—don't even see until the artist shows us the way." She peered at Marie-Christine over her book, as if seeking a response.

Marie-Christine felt as if she were falling into a newly painted world as vast as that black starry night outside. She slipped off the radiator. Annie's face was flushed too, her eyes still sparkled with excitement. "Annie Heaphy . . ." said Marie-Christine, as if tasting the name.

Annie looked puzzled.

Marie-Christine set down her red glass. She couldn't stop staring at this magnet of a woman—or understand her fascination. She reached trembling hands across the table and again caressed the ruddy cheeks. "I love your excitement."

Annie sipped wine, her eyes holding Marie-Christine's. "And what's yours? When you go looking for excitement—what do you find?"

Marie-Christine threw back her head and laughed. There was a string of many-colored beads between her breasts, and she took hold of the beads to roll between her fingers as she talked; her gold rings caught the light as did her earrings. "It's never been a philosopher-dyke before!"

She pulled her chair next to Annie. "Do you mind?" she

asked quickly, having forgotten they were not yet lovers. "I love sidewalk cafes. And maze-like museums. I love every kind of flower in the world. I love women. And adventure. Anything can be exciting to me. I particularly love watching ocean liners arrive and depart, I even check the *Times* for their schedules. Yesterday while I was walking at the docks I met a seventy-five-year-old sailor who'd just retired, and what he told me was this: no matter what port he sailed to, no matter what happened or who he met there, nothing was as exciting as pulling into port. New York has everything he longed for those years at sea, but none of it excites him because he's docked, he said, for good."

"You don't identify what you want? You just follow your will blindly like the old man and his ship?"

"Oh," said Marie-Christine, "I identify what I want. But I trust my will blindly to find it." Abruptly she asked, "You'll take me to bed now?"

Annie's eyes swept down her body. She seemed to be savoring it as she might one of her exciting ideas. She stood then, and caught Marie-Christine's hand as she passed her. "Would you like candles, or something?"

Marie-Christine lay back on a mattress raised slightly off the floor, arms lifted. "Please," she said, pulling Annie to her. "Do you think I'm awful? I've never wanted anyone this fast or hard. Annie, Annie Heaphy," she breathed as she held Annie and moved against her.

"You're very exciting, Marie-Christine," whispered Annie as she touched her lips that first time with her own. Marie-Christine was quivering. "Do you want to undress?"

"Yes."

Annie watched as Marie-Christine pulled off her jersey. "God, your breasts are beautiful," she said. She helped with her pants and boots. "God, you're beautiful all over."

"And you . . ." said Marie-Christine, kneeling before her. With one swift motion she unzipped the front of Annie's coveralls, expertly avoiding the pubic hair under her zipper. Before Annie could pull the coveralls off, Marie-Christine had slipped a hand between her legs and was spreading moisture everywhere. "You're still blonde there."

Annie knelt too, and touched those breasts. Marie-Christine slipped inside her, but Annie pulled away and gently pushed her down. "What would you like?" she asked.

"You be the artist. Show me your vision. Take me into your world. Your philosopher does acknowledge that lovers are artists?"

Annie seemed to hesitate, as if unsure her skills were equal to the challenge of this woman. But Marie-Christine had not stopped moving and Annie, lying against her, began to match her undulations. "You're incredible."

Marie-Christine could feel her vagina pulsate, as if seeking its own satisfaction. She wrapped one leg tightly around one of Annie's. She rubbed up and down the leg, shuddering.

"God," said Annie. Her hands and lips moved ceaselessly, as if also of their own will. She seemed to be trying to engulf Marie-Christine in even more sensations.

Then Marie-Christine's hold on her tightened. Tiny sounds like singing came from her throat. Annie just held her, cradling her orgasm.

"I felt as if you were all that contained me. If you hadn't held me I might have flown away."

Annie looked at her wondrously.

"Was I too forward for you? I'm not usually like this." Marie-Christine had turned all soft in her arms. The frizzy hair had become the curls of childhood, her smile one of supreme content.

"You are superb," said Annie Heaphy. "And no, you're not too forward. I want you again."

"Oh. I'm so glad it's not just me. Annie, what makes you so special? What do you do with your life besides driving cabs and reading philosophy?"

"I spend a lot of time at piano bars. I have every song Mabel Mercer ever recorded."

"Is there room for me in your life? Somewhere between Schopenhauer and Mabel Mercer?" Marie-Christine's hand was again between Annie's legs. She rolled Annie's inner lips between her fingers, back and forth, back and forth, slowly, hard.

"Room?" Annie almost squeaked.

"You feel like a delicate succulent. So good I have chills down my spine. May I taste you?"

"Oh, my gosh," said Annie, rolling weakly onto her back.

"Did I say something wrong?" Marie-Christine's mouth and tongue were already caressing Annie.

"Just exciting. I've never met anyone like—" But Marie-Christine had begun doing something new with her tongue and Annie was thrusting and rotating and tightening her thighs under Marie-Christine's splayed hands.

"You come fast," whispered Marie-Christine.

"Never," said Annie, obviously struggling for breath, "never that fast. Never like that."

"Then I'm good for you too?"

They were stretched flat against one another, thigh to thigh, stomach to stomach, breasts to breasts. Already their hands had begun to move again.

"Good?" Annie laughed, then answered in a kiss obviously meant to leave no question. For the first of many, many times, she reached to touch the electric pubic hair, to find the rosy labia, long and folding lovingly around her fingers. "That sailor?" murmured Annie as she kissed her way down Marie-Christine's body.

"Umm," answered Marie-Christine, lifting herself to meet Annie's lips, to hurry their contact.

"Poor guy. Not to have found an excitement like you."

Marie-Christine kept her eyes open, kept the star-filled window in sight. Here, in this cool stark room, were enough heat, enough flowers, enough light to last her a long long time.

Annie Heaphy appeared originally in the author's novel *Toothpick House*, 1984.

AT A BAR VI:*
WINTER SUN

It happened toward the end of the worst winter Sally the Bartender could remember. Other years had been colder, but you could dress to defend yourself against those; and there had certainly been stormier winters, when snow would fall and fall upon itself until it seemed it would seal shut the door of *Cafe Femmes* forever.

When had this particular winter begun to go wrong? Perhaps it was that heavy snow followed by a melt, then a freeze which left small glaciers stuck to streets and sidewalks.

"AT A BAR" I, II, III, IV, and V appeared in the author's short story collection *OLD DYKE TALES.* (1984)

People were still having accidents on that ice which had, like everything else left on the city's streets too long, turned filthy with grime. She stared at the ugly cold patches that seemed to keep winter anchored in New York. Sally had had enough.

Day after day her startled blue eyes squinted into the weak sun which dared to pit its powers against the ice. "Come on!" she felt like shouting, as if to a losing team. Then she'd have another drink from the bottle of red wine under the bar, to thaw her own impatience and anger at this standoff between the winter and the spring.

She couldn't quite remember when she'd switched from two glasses of white wine for special occasions to the red wine which seemed to flow so much more easily into her glass—and to disappear more quickly, more often. Come spring she'd switch back to the white. Or stop altogether. She'd watched too many fine gay kids go down under a flood of liquor which was supposed to ease their way. It wasn't even pretty any more, this warm red stuff that sometimes seemed sticky in the glass, and inside her was like clotting blood which clogged her veins. She didn't like, either, the way she and Liz had started bringing their drinking home. They had always drunk only at the bar—except for celebrations. Little by little, they seemed to celebrate more and more small things. First Sally thought it was because they were bored and needed to brighten their lives. But lately she feared that it was a need for the alcohol itself. Even on her own, she'd gotten into the habit of toasting the new day as soon as she got to work. Or having a quick one if she saw that queer-hating beer salesman, the one who shouldn't have a route anywhere near Greenwich Village, coming to do an order.

She wondered if he was the one behind the rumors that when federal funds became available to renovate the neighborhood, *Cafe Femmes* would be pushed out. Some lady from the art gallery up the street had filled her in when she'd come to get Sally and Liz to participate in the neighborhood association. The owners of the warehouse across the street wanted to convert their top floors into fancy co-op apartments, and having a gay bar in the neighborhood was not part of their plans. But Liz, who had an appointment with her father's lawyer, was certain they would be all right. They had toasted to their future in Soho.

A couple of kids came in to fortify themselves on their way somewhere else. She told them about the rumor and had a drink with them to toast *Cafe Femmes* remaining right where it was. When they left, smoke from their cigarettes hung in the air and she coughed till her throat hurt. Had it been months since she'd really breathed? Or years. . . . More and more often she scared herself wondering about things like that, worrying about her increasing sensitivity to what she and Liz called "occupational hazards." Hell, she thought, it'll be better next month when we can open the door. What, after all, could she and Liz do which was anything like running a gay bar?

The cowbells clanged and she felt a quick surge of irritation. Those bells had been cute at first, a friendly warning that one of the kids was coming through the door. But now—sometimes she wished the kids would stay out, especially those who drank in the mornings, who couldn't get through the day without a drink.

But it was only Gabby. She'd given the stuff up a while back and came in now just because she could be herself at *Cafe Femmes*. As she watched Gabby take a stool, Sally couldn't help but remember when Meg had fallen down several flights of stairs, drunk, and how Gabby had run to her aid. She'd visited for hours at a time in the hospital, then had found the job she still had to earn rent money for both of them. Meg had been drunk for so long that she'd had no health insurance, and injured, she hadn't the stamina to apply for city welfare, much less subsist on it. Gabby had learned by Meg's mistake, had stopped drinking and hung onto the job, even when Meg became well enough to walk to a bar, a liquor store—and did. "Never," Gabby had said at *Cafe Femmes* the night she discovered Meg's backsliding, "I'm *never* going to get like that. I want you to kill me first, Sal, if you ever catch me with a drink."

Sally shook her blonde hair out of her eyes and wiped down the bar with a wet rag. "What are you doing out of work so early?" she asked Gabby.

Gabby didn't answer right away. Her eyes were hidden by overgrown bangs, her chunky fists beat a nervous rhythm against the bar. Finally she looked up, not at Sally, but behind the bar, at the bottles.

Sally felt a constriction in her chest, as if the sweet red wine had gotten stuck inside her heart.

"What've you got good?" asked Gabby, looking half-challengingly, half-coyly out from under her bangs.

Sally was silent. She wasn't going to help.

"How about some of that Wild Turkey?" Gabby suggested as if she were kidding.

But Sally saw the dead-serious determination to have a drink. "What happened?" she asked tonelessly, not moving.

The sun had disappeared behind a cloud and the bar looked dingy. Gabby's cold-reddened cheeks were fading to the same pasty-white color most of the kids at *Cafe Femmes* wore these days. "Gabby," prompted Sally.

"I got fired," her friend mumbled.

"Oh, no."

"It wasn't my fault this time, I swear," Gabby said quickly.

"I didn't say it was. But you kept this job so long. What happened?" There was a feeling of doom about *Cafe Femmes* today which made her shudder. Maybe it really didn't belong in this neighborhood. Gabby had tried so hard to keep the job. When she'd stopped drinking Sally had somehow assumed life would get better for her.

"You've seen me bring Sue here. She's the bi girl I work with?"

Sally nodded.

"This new foreman came on and he started dating her too."

Sally sighed. She knew what had happened. "Didn't Sue stick up for you?"

"Maybe, I don't know. Why should she risk her neck for me anyways? She's got one foot in the safe camp."

How many times had Sally heard this story? She groaned. Gabby looked up at her, surprised, and Sally realized that she'd sounded like an animal in pain.

It was the conflict hurting her so much inside. For months it had been getting more and more clear to Sally that she had to decide what was right for her. Yes, it felt good to be with gay kids all the time. And yes, the kids needed a place to be together, to be away from straights and guys, a place where they wouldn't be stared at or laughed at or thrown out for being themselves, a place to go when they'd been fired. But was *Cafe Femmes* the best place for them?

Spending so much time in a bar, they naturally drank. When you drank, it was beginning to dawn on Sally, you drank more. She'd always had her doubts about that part of running a bar. She and Liz had talked about it off and on, especially lately, as both of them watched their "kids" get older and drink more. They'd been feeling worse and worse about pouring the stuff.

"Are we any better than pushers on a corner?" Sally had asked Liz one painful Monday, their day off, as they walked their aging dog Spot along the East River.

"Of course," rationalized Liz, "these people don't *O.D.* on booze."

"They don't?" Sally stopped and faced Liz, all too aware of her own hangover. As they searched each other's eyes Sally remembered this one, or that one, who got sick, who disappeared, who got put away.

Spot had tugged at her leash. They'd dropped the subject again. Sally couldn't imagine leaving the bar. How could she ever fit into an office again? Besides, the bar had been Liz's dream.

So this pain, then escaping now in a groan, had been corroding her insides, doing as much damage, she imagined, as the liquor she drank to soothe it. She searched for her wine. What else could she do?

"Hey—customers first," said Gabby.

Sally poured her own. Her pain disappeared as she drank. Then she wiped the bar down again and poured Gabby a mixture of seltzer and grape juice, dressing it up with a slice of lime, a slice of orange and plenty of crushed ice.

"What is this shit?" Gabby demanded.

"My newest blend." Sally turned her back and pretended to be busy.

"Hey, Sal. Pal. *You* don't give it to me and I'll go someplace else."

Sally's pain returned. She picked up her wine, then set it down; to drink it would just be rubbing it in. "I can't, Gab."

"Why the hell not?"

"I don't want to get you started drinking again."

"It's my life."

"It's *my friend's* life."

Gabby's face was red with anger. "Friend? I just got fired. I *need* a damn drink. A *friend* would give it to me."

As usual, Sally was calm. "Not the way I see it."

"So save all the other kids. Why pick on me?"

"I'm not the Salvation Army. I'm just one gay bartender."

"Then maybe you ought to go *join* the Salvation Army and not *be* a bartender."

Sally wanted that wine. So what if she rubbed it in? No, that would make Gabby mad enough to go someplace else and get it. Clearly, the only thing to do was to give her the stuff. But how could she?

The Wild Turkey was so seldom used it was dusty. Too expensive for these kids. "One," she said, "on the house. Just to show you how much you hate it." She pushed the shot glass toward Gabby and slammed the bottle back on the shelf, still dirty. She hated it. She hated all the bottles and never wanted to make them sparkle in the sunlight of *Cafe Femmes'* window again.

Gabby downed it, choked, then sighed. Sally knew that warm feeling of release, of relaxation. She reached for her wine as Gabby pushed the shot glass and a five across the bar, looking warily up at her.

That groan came out of Sally again. Her hand stayed on the neck of the wine bottle. "I said one," she growled.

"What's the matter, Sal, feeling guilty about feeding our habits all of a sudden? Don't push your guilt on me."

Sally's rage warmed her veins. She needed no wine. As a matter of fact, she needed much more than wine, and she knew just what it was she needed to do. Fearfully, trembling, she began.

Slowly, she lifted the wine bottle high above the bar, lifted it till the bottle began to spill its stream of red onto the floor, lifted it as if to empty it and then, then—smashed it on the edge of the bar.

Gabby stared at her in horror.

Sally held the jagged neck toward Gabby. "I'll smash a bottle every time you take a drink." Then she lifted the Wild Turkey off the shelf and filled the shot glass.

Gabby hesitatingly put it to her lips. She sipped, her eyes

glued to Sally as if searching for her calm, slow-moving ways.

Sally smashed the Wild Turkey bottle. She threw both bottle necks to the floor and reached blindly for another bottle.

"Sal," said Gabby, rising, glass in hand.

"Drink, you ass!"

Gabby, as if hypnotized, drank.

Sally smashed the next bottle, a clear white rum. This time she cut her hand. Blood ran onto the next bottle she picked up.

Gabby put her glass down, then snatched it up quickly, as if to fortify herself.

SMASH, went the blood-smeared bottle.

Gabby threw her glass across the bar and moved back slowly, cautiously, from her stool toward the door.

"Going to another bar?" snarled Sally.

Gabby nodded.

SMASH.

Gabby put her hand on the doorknob.

SMASH.

"You're crazy," said Gabby.

"Finally," said Sally.

Gabby slipped out the door.

The cowbells echoed over and over in Sally's ears. She drowned them out by throwing a bottle of blackberry brandy at the mirror over the bar. A long crack appeared in the reflection of *Cafe Femmes*. Sally wanted to methodically smash every bottle in the bar, but she wasn't feeling methodical.

It must have been a call from Gabby that brought Liz so quickly, in a cab. Except to chase out a kid looking for a drink, Sally had been playing pinball all that time, paper towels wrapped around her cut hand. Through the window she saw Liz, Gabby, and the kid, staring in at her.

"Listen, I'm sorry," Sally said as the anxious group entered. "I guess I went a little nuts."

Liz was behind the bar already, moaning, "Oy, oy, oy," her hands to her head as she surveyed the damage.

Gabby, standing gingerly a long way from Sally, stared at her.

"Want another one?" Sally asked her. She was crying now, her long body slumped against the pinball machine.

Liz went to her, wringing her hands, looking close into Sally's face. "What is it? What happened? You decided you don't want the business any more?"

"Gabby's drinking again."

"It's all *my* fault?" Gabby objected, pointing at herself emphatically with her thumbs.

Liz glared at Gabby. "You stay out of this." She turned back to Sally. "So Gabby's a fool. You have to be one too?"

Sally's whole demeanor conveyed defeat. "Maybe we should let the neighborhood association push us out," she said. "Maybe they're right and we don't deserve to exist at all. What's so damn foolish about being sick and tired of watching our friends turn into alcoholics?"

"I'm no alcoholic!" protested Gabby.

Liz glared again, and the kid steered Gabby to a table by the window.

"This is your fault, that they drink like fish?"

"Come on, Liz." Sally was standing, her shoulders stooped with misery. "You know what I mean. We've talked about it enough."

Liz surveyed the damage pointedly. "We never talked about tearing down with our bare hands what it took so long to build."

Sally hung her head. "I said I was sorry."

"Oh, Sal," Liz said, taking her in her arms. "I'm sorry too. We should have talked more. Done something. You need some time off."

"Time off? How about forever?"

"I think that's a terrible solution," said Liz, leading her to another table by the window.

Sally felt the tears well up again. Never again to watch the seasons pass outside this window? Never again to stay open Christmas Day so that the kids would all have someplace to go? Never again to hear another sad story and watch it all turn out right? Never to realize their dream of running a lesbian bar with a difference—a gay bar that *cared?*

"I've been thinking about alternatives, Sally." Liz had a list before her. "I've been carrying this around, adding ideas as I ride the subway."

Sally clenched her fists. "We could turn it into a straight bar and watch *them* become alcoholics."

Liz tapped a foot. "*That's* not on my list. You want to hear this or not?"

Someone tried the door. Sally could see it was the two women who'd toasted *Cafe Femmes* staying in the neighborhood.

"Gabby," Liz said, "find the closed sign in all this mess, will you?"

"What'll I tell those two outside?"

Liz looked at Sally. "Tell them we're making alterations," Liz said. "Tell them not to go away forever."

Gabby bustled till she found the sign, then strode to the door as if she carried the fate of the kingdom to the crowds. When she shut the door she said, "They say to hurry, this is the nicest dive in town. And if the neighborhood gives you any trouble they'll help you fight back."

Sally's eyes met Liz's.

Her voice heavy, Liz began her list. "A juice bar."

"They don't make money."

"A game parlor."

"Just what I always wanted. To wear a change apron."

"A restaurant." Liz looked particularly attentive, waiting for Sally's response.

"Why don't we get a Lavender Julie franchise?" Sally answered sarcastically.

"You're being negative."

"You know what the failure rate is for restaurants."

"Not when they're part of an established bar."

"I guess I just don't really want to close *Cafe Femmes.*"

"Close *Cafe Femmes?*" shouted Gabby, rising and striding to their table. "What would we do without *Cafe Femmes?*" Ignoring Liz's look, she went on, "You're burnt out, Sal, that's all. We *need* this place. You guys are doing us good, not harm. Think about it."

Gabby looked so earnest, had such an air of proprietorship, that Sally had to laugh. "First off, I said I *didn't* want to close *Cafe Femmes.*"

Gabby lowered her gaze and sunk her hands into the pockets of her corduroys.

"Second," Sally continued, "without *Cafe Femmes* you'd be drunk by now."

"See?" said Liz.

"Yeah." Sally replied, smiling for the first time all day. "But look what I had to go through to keep her sober!"

"I'm sorry, Sal," said Gabby. "I was just feeling low. You were right. I really didn't need the drink. I guess I need to *be* here, not drink here. It's just," she flung her short arms out helplessly, "you know how hard it is for me to get a job someplace where I fit in."

More women came to the door and Liz motioned for the kid to take care of them.

"And third," Sally said, stretching her long legs out from under the table, "you're right. I need time off. Lots of it. I need something more," she said, turning to Liz, "than the bar and walking Spot on Mondays with you."

In a soft tone devoid of expression Liz asked, "Do you want to be the *Cafe Femmes* representative to the Neighborhood Association?"

Sally looked at her in amazement. "I thought we didn't want anything to do with that bunch."

"Today was the day I met with the lawyer."

Liz seemed so thoughtful that Sally had a moment of fear. What *would* she do without *Cafe Femmes?* "I forgot. What did he say?"

Liz spoke absently, as if continuing an internal conversation. "I've been trying to figure out where we'd get the time. My first thought when I saw you like that today was, 'How am I going to handle this too?' But you may just be the solution."

"I feel more like the problem."

"He advised us not only to participate in the Neighborhood Association, but to become important in it. Show them we have something to give the street. Something unique."

"Like me!" Gabby burst out, doing a little tap dance. She was obviously growing excited.

Liz laughed, then leaned forward. "Sally, we *are* unique. We're the only bar on the street. We're the only gay business. We bring people *into* the neighborhood who otherwise would never come here. They buy from the pizza place. From other little shops. And we're the only establishment that serves a completely *social* function."

"So?"

"So? Oh, boy!" said Gabby. "Don't you see? What a lunkhead you can be, Sally James. You could be the—what do you call it? In the middle of everything!"

"The fulcrum," said Liz.

"Yes. The whatever it is. You could have meetings in your back room. You could do a lot of extra stuff with all the time you spend alone in here, in this time off you want. You could sponsor a softball team!"

"She's right, Sally. Most of the people are pefectly willing for us to stay. But with a real place in the community, they'd need us, want us here, and the people who don't like us would lose any power they had to hurt us."

"A gay bar? They'd want a *gay* bar?"

"No. They'd want *Cafe Femmes*. A cafe. The way I've always dreamed it would be. With coffee, sandwiches, French pastries, along with the liquor. And tables on the sidewalk—just a few—with pretty tablecloths under an awning."

There was silence in *Cafe Femmes* as if the very building was astonished to think of itself all prettied up like that. The kid lounged at the door. Gabby stared at Liz.

Sally asked, still skeptical, "Can we afford it? For me to work less hours and to get the licenses we'd need, the equipment, the furnishings?"

"If we keep it simple, try to retain the same feeling we have. The awning would be the biggest expense, but we could have our name printed on it and forget about the neon sign we were planning. And, because we're improving the business, I think we can get a low-interest loan from the neighborhood development people. Best of all, we can write everything off, including your salary for working on the improvements."

Liz paused, breathed deeply, then waited for Sally's response. Gabby nobly controlled her excitement, betraying it only with occasional jingles of the change in her pocket.

"What color?" asked Sally.

Gabby was suddenly still.

"What color is what?" asked Liz.

"The awning."

Liz smiled. Sally smiled. Their eyes locked as they reached to hold each other's hands across the table. Liz peeled the paper towel from Sally's cut. It had stopped bleeding.

Into the silence Gabby's excited words sounded like a

cannon shot: "Lavender!"

"Oh, no," said Sally, dropping her head into her hands. "It *is* a Lavender Julius."

Liz laughed. "We're going trendy!"

"Not very," cautioned Sally.

"No, not very with Gabby tending bar and running the food counter."

"Gabby?" asked Sally, as if trying on the idea.

"Gabby?" asked Gabby. Then, quickly, "*Me?*"

"You said you needed a job," Sally reminded her.

Gabby whirled in place. "Gabby-the-bartender!" she cried. "This calls for a celebration!"

Sally looked suspiciously toward her.

Gabby flushed red. "Not Wild Turkey."

"There *is* no Wild Turkey," Sally said sternly.

"What you made me before," Gabby explained, licking her lips. "With the lime? And the crushed ice? And the orange?"

Sally rose, smiling.

"Only, Sal," asked Gabby nervously, "would you add *one* other thing?"

Sally hovered threateningly. "No liq—"

"Would you put a *cherry* in it too?"

AT A BAR VII:
THE FLORIST SHOP

The bar was closed for two days that week. One for repairs, the other to give them a real day off. On that second day Sally and Liz felt so rested that they woke at dawn.

Just to rise so early in the morning gave shivers of excitement to Sally. On Mondays they often lingered in bed together, long blonde Sally and soft dark-haired Liz, enjoying rubbing against one another under the tangled sheets, reprieved from the usual tearing apart from each other to enter the day.

It wasn't that they had grown weary of running *Cafe Femmes*. Sally still enjoyed the daily subway ride downtown to just below the Village, where she would find the warehouse district long awake, working at a pace that seemed designed to bring the lunch hour on even sooner.

But today they were on their own, adventures before them. They had nothing in particular planned, yet before they'd said a word Sally was kicking the covers off her long legs and pulling Liz up with her into the shower where they quickly washed, and more slowly made love, before bursting out of their apartment building into the sunlight. The crisp spring morning was delicious, the sun was bright enough to throw sharp shadows everywhere; they passed from the cavernous darkness of tall buildings to the glory of a circle of yellow daffodils in Central Park, and warmed up with the morning as they crossed the Park and found delicious blueberry muffins, crusted with sugar, in a little coffee shop on 61st Street.

By ten o'clock the uptown boutiques were opening and grey-suited businesspeople raced one another into and out of the buildings. Sally and Liz had walked off the heaviness of their meal, but they'd begun to tire just a little.

"Do you want to go back to the Park?" asked Liz.

"Or to a museum?" asked Sally.

"See a movie?" But they shook their heads no to that. Who'd want to spend the whole afternoon inside on a day like today?

"The Cloisters," Liz suggested.

"Too far," answered Sally.

"Gallery-hopping!"

They agreed, laughing, and turned back to Madison Avenue. Once before, just because they'd found themselves in the neighborhood, they'd invented a game in which they were rich and snobbish art buyers. In their jeans and Cafe Femmes jackets, looking like refugees from a softball team, they'd taken the galleries by storm. This painting wasn't quite right for the sunken living room, that photograph would look gorgeous by the door to the penthouse patio.

Anything under forty thousand was cheap, anything over, pretentious.

"We may get kicked out this time," warned Sally.

"With our chutzpah? Who would dare?"

"Look at the flowers!" cried Sally. She set their course for a spot bright with color half a block away. "I'll buy you some and no one will be able to tell you from a lady!"

Liz looked over her glasses, eyebrows together in a stern frown. "And ain't I a lady?" She was doing her Barbra Streisand imitation.

"Of course you are," laughed Sally, stopping to nuzzle Liz in broad daylight. "But you're *my* kind of lady, thank goodness, not theirs."

Mollified, Liz nuzzled back. "Do I see violets?" she whispered.

They both sighed. Sally felt a shiver like the one she'd had that morning. Violets had been their flower the night they admitted their love.

From a cart outside the florist shop, Liz chose a bouquet of yellow daffodils, their flower of the day, and Sally went inside to pay.

"Sally!"

She looked up. She struggled to recall the face before her. But it wasn't the slack-muscled face with its heavy eyebrows that she remembered first, it was the feel of the woman. Tall and ungainly, as if she'd once been heavy and had never got used to losing weight. She exuded hurt.

"Julie!" She turned to Liz. "Remember? The girl from Jersey whose first lover—" She hesitated to say it.

"Killed herself," Julie finished in a flat tone. "I got over that, with your help. I could see how it was for her, everybody telling her how great straight was when inside all she wanted was gay."

"Yes," Liz said, "I remember well. I'm glad you're doing better."

"Hey, it's been what, almost two years now. I hope I grew up some."

"What're you doing here?" Sally asked.

"I manage the place."

"Great. You move into the city?"

"Not at first." Julie moved to her work table. "I have some orders to get out," she explained, and placed six faintly pink carnations on wrapping paper, along with six fluffy white ones. "Remember the cleaners I worked at in Jersey? The owner's brother has half a dozen flower stores. We got to talking one day and I told him about me and flowers." She smiled and shrugged, glancing, Sally noticed, past them and out the window. "I guess you wouldn't take me for the type, but that's always been my thing. Learned it from my mother, how to grow flowers. She has seventeen varieties of roses in our backyard, and that's just roses."

Again she peered past them out the window. Was that how she checked on customers at the carts? "He'd heard about my troubles, about losing my friend and being depressed and all, so he offered me a job here. It wasn't as manager, not right away. I was the helper."

Sally could see now that Julie was looking beyond the carts and up a little. Sunlight blanketed the yellow, red, and purple flowers outside, but the shop was chilly. "I loved it from the start, handling the flowers, meeting new people who didn't remind me of anything in my life. A lot of secretaries come in here all the time to order flowers and we talk. Some of them are even gay." She flashed a frankly proud smile. "I don't hide it now, you know. Not since I saw what that can do to people, being scared of what they are."

But that hurt look had returned as she spoke, like the first time Julie had come to the bar, lost and bitter and alone. Sally recalled how just that one day's connection with other gays had turned Julie around, let her lose her anger at the world for pushing her girl into suicide, for silencing her own pain as a lover.

Julie finished wrapping the order and stepped to a refrigerated case to choose some flowers Sally didn't recognize. Liz had slipped her hand into Sally's, squeezing tightly as if frightened or uneasy. As soon as Julie returned to the work table she looked up and out again across to the shaded side of the street.

"To make a long story short I did move into the city, into a studio apartment across the Park. And since I didn't know anybody—I'm still not good at making friends—I hung around the shop. I used to walk all over the city too, getting ideas how to display our flowers, what better services we could offer, you know, building business. The owner liked my ideas so much he gave me the store to manage after only a year." She finished her arrangement and looked up at them, then quickly back down, like a person begging for approval. "So here I am, talking your heads off again."

"It's a nice shop," said Liz. "Clean and bright." But still her cold hand clung to Sally's.

Julie was looking outside. "It's got to be. On Madison Avenue we wouldn't sell a thing if we didn't fit in."

Sally turned to look out the window. All up and down the street were tall grey and glass buildings, mostly newly built. But directly across the street there was a hole in the frontage, a wreckers' ball hanging over the cavity. The first floor of an older building was all that remained standing. Was it this that fascinated Julie? The desolate picture of a wreckers' ball poised to finish its destruction? "What was that building?" she asked.

All three looked to where Julie had gazed. "Just an old office building nobody wanted anymore. They fought for years to keep it standing, but some big company finally won out." She paused as if uncertain whether to go on.

Her heavy brows were pulled forward as if she were in pain. Liz squeezed tight on Sally's hand.

"I guess you caught me at a bad time again," Julie explained. "Things were going so good, too." She bit her lip and nodded toward the wreckers' ball. "I met a girl. She worked there. Every Friday she'd order flowers for her boss's girlfriend."

Across the street, in the plate glass window to the left of the dying building, Sally could just barely see a reflection of the flower carts, all distorted.

Julie said, "She was only a gal Friday. And she wasn't pretty or anything, but maybe that's why I liked her. Curly was so different from my first girl. I guess I thought she was tougher, could take the gay life better. That she'd be safe for me to love. She practically lived at my place the last couple months. We were always together."

Lunch hour must have passed as they talked, because men were drifting back onto the demolition site. Someone climbed into the cab below the wreckers' ball. The sun had shifted; it fell straight down onto Madison Avenue, between the flower shop and the remains of the condemned building.

"I knew she wouldn't be around forever anyway. She was saving money to go to school somewhere out of town where she could live cheap."

A customer came in and Julie was transformed. Smiling, she became a thoroughly professional saleswoman. The man left with an Easter lily for his mother *and* a quickly assembled corsage for his wife. "That's how you've got to be to keep the profits up," Julie said, as if embarrassed to reveal her other side. Her features slackened into melancholy as her gaze returned to the window.

"Her boss announced that the building was going to be torn down. Curly came across to tell me. It was pouring cats and dogs and she was soaked. Her hair," she laughed quietly, "always got frizzy then, like little flowers curling up in the dark. She said as long as the job was going, she thought it was time for her to move on. Two weeks later she was gone. To some school in Ohio where she had relatives."

Sally tried to think of something to say, but only managed to go on squeezing Liz's hand.

Outside, the ball had begun to rise on its heavy cable. Julie looked more lost and helpless than ever. "Why do I always get myself into these dead-end relationships?" The ball struck once, then again and again. A shudder seemed to pass through Julie's body with each blow.

"Maybe you guys showing up in my life again is a sign. Maybe I have to make another change. Do you think I should follow Curly to Ohio?" Her eyes swept the little shop, its flowers, its shininess, its stack of orders on the table. "Since I got here we had to add another refrigerator to handle all the new stock I sell every day."

They watched her lay ferns against paper, set flowers deftly into place, wrap them up. She stapled cards to each batch and placed them in a filling cooler.

Sally was desperate to be back out on the street. Here was Julie stuck again, this time in a world of her own making. She'd surrounded herself with dying flowers and synthetic light, and now stared fascinated at a wreckers' ball. As if that weren't bad enough, virtually the only lesbians she'd met in two years just happened to walk into her shop. Hadn't she learned anything that first time?

"How come you never come by *Cafe Femmes?*"

Julie looked at them both, then out the window. "I never have time, with the store and all."

"It's spring out there, Julie," Sally said, concealing her impatience with difficulty.

Julie looked hurt by her tone. She finished another bouquet. "I kind of lose track of the seasons. In here it's always spring."

"Or never spring," Sally said.

Liz dropped Sally's hand. "New York City is the gay capital of the world," she said gently.

"You mean I should get out into the spring and meet people." She drew her brows together again. "But what about Curly?"

A crumpling sound drew all their eyes to the window at the same moment. The building was down. Nothing was left of the form it had been but rubble.

"I guess that's just an excuse." Julie laughed derisively. "You know what I just thought of? I must've thought I was safe as could be tucked away in my little shop on Madison Avenue. Maybe no place is safe. I was hiding, and what good did it do me?"

Sally had put the demolished building out of her mind; she simply looked longingly toward the sun on the wreckers' side of the street.

"Hey," Julie said. "I don't want to keep you from where you're going. Listen, how about tomorrow night? Can I deliver you some flowers at the bar? When will you both be there? I can have my helper close up for me for once."

Sally and Liz exchanged smiles. "Around seven. And consider those flowers a standing order," said Sally, as they drifted toward the door. "Once a week—at least."

AT A BAR VIII:
THE LONG SLOW–BURNING FUSE

Sometimes, as she watched the slow, subtly changing seasons through the plate glass window, Sally the Bartender could barely contain her excitement. Today, it was as if beneath her bad mood there was a long, slow-burning fuse inside her that just would *not* explode, and she moved restlessly about, cleaning, serving, stocking, wiping down the bar with a fervor more suitable to dancing or Olympic racing.

Even Gabby wasn't around to tease and cajole her out of her mood; she'd worked Thursday and Friday while Sally had run around the city applying for a neighborhood renovation loan and for licenses to serve food at *Cafe Femmes*. The same cab driver who'd been stopping by to play pinball all week was at it again today, the only customer in the bar. Sally had never seen her before this week, but her cab was parked out front again and she was becoming a fixture.

It had been a dim Saturday morning. Just about the time the cabbie arrived the sun broke loose as if running toward spring and made the street warmer than it had been for months. Sally had switched then, from mineral water to Seven-Up, remembering how, when she'd been sick as a child and her mother had brought it to her, all bubbly and sweet and dry-tasting, it had always made her feel better.

"Quarters," said the cabbie, coming up to the bar. The accent was Boston. "Jeeze, it really *is* spring," she added, looking out at the street.

Sally had propped open the door of *Cafe Femmes*, and a bunch of kids from Little Italy were rolling by on skates.

Sally wasn't encouraging any conversation today. She nodded. Up close, she could see that the cabbie was nearly her age. She wore olive chinos, a grey sweatshirt with sleeves pushed up to the elbow, and a tweed cap.

Sally's grumpiness seemed to subside a little with her curiosity, and with the bright warm day.

"You're never on at night," the cabbie said, lingering.

"No," Sally answered, her voice feeling rusty from disuse. So the cabbie was a night customer too.

"What is it that Gabby drinks at night, with all the stuff in it?"

"Grape juice and seltzer. With, let's see, slices of orange, lime, a cherry and plenty of crushed ice."

"Let me have one of those, okay? I have to go back to work soon and I don't want to smell like I've been here."

"One Lavender Julie coming up," said Sally.

The cabbie laughed. Sally joined her. Why, after all, should she hold onto her mood? Just because the woman Liz had had that quick hot affair with in Paris had moved to New York? Just because Liz had spoken of Marie-Christine for years as if she could walk on water? Just because the woman had made magic with Liz's body in a way Liz had never forgotten? Just because, lately, there had been an excitement about Liz way beyond what a renovation scheme should inspire?

As she got older, she had learned, deep in one season, to recognize the signs of the next. In winter, this winter, she'd been rejoicing in each extra moment of light added to the end of each afternoon. And in Liz, with each new season she anticipated the next and the next spent together. As if Liz, restless with restrained enthusiasm as she arrived for her shift at *Cafe Femmes,* were the source of all this new light, not the more and more reluctantly setting sun. Sally loved Liz in their eighth year more and more passionately than ever. But was Liz restless, stirred by memories and ready to enter a new season in her life?

"How much do I owe you for the Lavender Julie?" asked the cabbie.

"I don't know," Sally said, returning to the present. "I never sold one before. Since it's my first, it's on the house." She smiled despite herself. "To encourage you not to drink and drive."

"Don't worry about that. I like my job. I want to keep it."

Sally wiped down the bar and poured herself some Seven-Up. They sat companionably, gazing out the window and the open door.

"There's something about this place," said the cabbie. "When I started seeing my lover a year ago I stopped going to any but piano bars. But I missed *Cafe Femmes.* So I decided to take my lunch hour here. I don't get to be with many dykes in my business. The ones who can afford cab fare can't afford to look like dykes, so I don't know who they are."

"Why don't you bring your girl down here?"

The cabbie took her hat off, then set it on her head again. "I don't know. I guess I thought she'd like a classier place. But now that I know her better, maybe I will." She swiveled her stool to look at Sally. "You and Gabby own this?"

Sally shook her head. "Liz and me. The other bartender. Gabby's just a friend." She laughed. "A regular who turned into a permanent."

"She tells me you're going to serve food."

"A sidewalk cafe. Liz got the idea for a lesbian bar on a graduation trip to Europe. But we couldn't afford to make it into more than this." She indicated the small dark space with her arm. "Now, with a neighborhood association and federal money, we can't afford not to."

"My lover might like a sidewalk cafe. She grew up over in Europe."

The skaters clambered by in the opposite direction. One fell, laughing; the others picked her up. The long-skirted woman who operated the art gallery up the street walked by, waving, then stuck her head through the open door. "Beautiful day!" she called.

The cabbie stood. "I have time for one last game. Want to play?"

Sally liked this woman. She seemed sure of herself and affable, easy. Unlike so many of the lesbians who came in, she wasn't much of a drinker and appeared to know who she was and what she wanted in life. And she seemed comfortable, as if she belonged right where she was. "Okay," she said.

The cabbie held out a hand; her girp was warm, steady. "The name's Annie. Annie Heaphy."

* * * * *

When Sally left *Cafe Femmes* that night she dreaded
going home. There were just so many things she could discuss
with Spot, the dog, and after that she knew she'd begin to
brood about Liz again. She called a neighbor to walk and
feed the dog, then went over to her favorite restaurant in
Little Italy. She ordered her usual dish of linguine with a rich
red sauce.

But thoughts of Liz and Marie-Christine invaded her as
if her mind were a battlefield. Maybe Liz *was* seeing her
again. And so what if she was? That didn't mean that what
they had this time would be good. Look what had happened
with Roxy. The affair that had flared up between Sally and
her had lasted no more than three months and had disappeared so quickly it hadn't left a dent in her life with Liz.
As long as Liz got it over with fast and didn't leave, she
thought she could take it. But if she found so much as one
curly blonde hair on their pillows, ever. . . . She bit savagely
into a hunk of garlic bread.

Half an hour of twirling the delicate homemade linguine
on her fork and savoring the sauce on her tongue calmed her.
She ordered a cream-filled pastry and a white creme de
menthe. She could always console herself with food if Liz
left, after all. She was beginning to feel a little guilty because
she hadn't told Liz she was staying downtown. All she had to
do was go home now and it wouldn't matter, she wouldn't
feel as if she was sneaking around checking up on Liz. But
when she paid her bill and strolled around the neighborhood
awhile to help her digestion, she spotted a movie theater. The
film would be over by ten-thirty. It would be the most
natural thing, then, to stop by the bar.

The hero's name was not Marie-Christine, but he was tall
and blonde like her. He was not French-speaking Swiss like
Marie-Christine, but he was suave and debonair as she must
be. Marie-Christine: butchy, with the graceful hands of a lover,
the manners of a royal prince, swaying over a woman—her

Liz!—on a dance floor. The hero, the successful seducer. The *cad*, she cursed to herself, folding her arms and slumping down sulkily in her molded plastic theater seat.

* * * * *

When she left the movie theater and walked back to *Cafe Femmes*, the warehouses were shut down, silently ranged along the dark street. If she could only store her heart as the businesses of the city stored their goods. Pad it, box it, till she was certain it wouldn't bruise.

She could hear noise at *Cafe Femmes* long before she reached it. After all, it was a Saturday night. Saturday night in New York City and Liz was enjoying herself with. . . .

The music was so loud she could barely hear the cowbells as she opened the door against them. *Cafe Femmes* was packed.

"Am I glad to see you," said Liz as Sally moved quickly behind the bar to help her. "I've been trying to get you or Gabby down here for hours. Hours! I think it was the spring weather that brought everyone out tonight."

She couldn't believe it. Was everything all right after all? As she worked, she scanned the crowd suspiciously. No sign of anyone with blonde curly hair. Perhaps she'd dyed it. In any case, it felt so good to be home, with the pinball machine sounding its buzzers and bells, the cigarette smoke filling the room and her nostrils like a cloud of Saturday night excitement made visible, the kids laughing, talking, arguing, dancing to the blaring jukebox—but most of all Liz, dear Liz moving around her and with her to the same rhythms they'd always moved to. Her heart peeped out of its warehouse, drawn by the warmth of love.

But then the cowbells on the door jangled rudely and there she was, a tall woman with blonde curly hair, looking at Liz as if she'd just been presented with the world on a silver platter—and expected it.

"Marie-Christine!" cried Liz, rushing into her arms.

Sally's heart, retreating as fast as it could, still felt a rent begin.

"Hi there, Sally-the-Bartender," said the woman who'd entered with Marie-Christine. She was shorter, wore a tweed cap. It was Annie Heaphy, the cabbie. "I guess they know each other," she said, grinning.

"You?" Sally said in astonishment. "You and Marie-Christine?" She was staring at Marie-Christine in her mauve woolen cape, long gold earrings, stylishly baggy pants, high boots, and an orange silken scarf around her crazy curly yellow hair.

"You know her too?"

"No. I mean—" Sally couldn't stop herself from saying, "I thought she was butch."

Annie laughed. "Marie-Christine butch?" She shook her head. "Sometimes," she whispered loudly over the crowd, "she's so femme I think she's a transvestite."

Sally laughed with her, but mostly in relief. She began to work again and Liz joined her, radiant. "Did you see who's here?" Liz asked.

"I noticed a little commotion," said Sally calmly, as if the commotion hadn't taken place in her heart.

Marie-Christine, in her charming accent, ordered a bottle of champagne for the occasion. Sally was entranced by her large blue eyes, her style—but she couldn't imagine why *Liz* had fallen for her.

"What happened in Paris?" she asked Liz during a lull. "Was she your type then?"

"Oh, no," Liz said, laughing. "But then Paris was another world. I was another woman. My head was turned by everything over there. I was captivated by all the women. And," Liz's mouth went soft, her eyes sultry, "she was expert in bed."

Sally looked Marie-Christine over once more. For all the times she'd heard of the woman's expertise, she'd never quite imagined herself intrigued by it.

Liz paused and thought a moment. "But then I'd only been to bed with a straight college girl. I hadn't even met you yet." She gave a little jump for joy and then went into high gear filling orders again. "It's so good to see her. Like finding a dear old friend."

"And this is the first time you've seen her?"

Liz raised her eyebrows as if surprised. "I've only talked on the phone with her once, last month, briefly. She gave me her number, but I haven't been able to find it again since."

Annie was at the bar, ordering another Lavender Julie. "Marie-Christine ate all the fruit out of my first," she explained, shrugging. She said disappointedly, "I don't know if we can get near your pinball machine tonight."

Marie-Christine slid onto the stool beside Annie.

Sally offered, "I'll tell the kids it's reserved for you between midnight and one."

"Oh, no!" Marie-Christine laughed. "We can wait our turn. I want to talk with you, too, and with Liz. My Annie says she's been haunting your bar. Since we met she's been telling me it's her favorite, but would never bring me here. It's true you're making it into a restaurant with outdoor tables?"

There was something about Marie-Christine, like Annie Heaphy, that made Sally comfortable. But with Marie-Christine she also felt a stirring of the long slow fuse inside her. She tore her eyes from the woman's face and noticed her hand nestled, moving, deep in the crotch of Annie's pants. "Yes," Sally stammered, embarrassed.

Annie sat, coolly, squeezing her thighs against Marie-Christine's hand to the rhythm of the music.

"Would you like a suggestion?" Marie-Christine asked. "If they were my outdoor tables?"

Liz had reappeared to draw a draft. "Yes, yes," she said, "but wait till I can hear it!"

"Marie-Christine studied art history in Paris," said Annie. "You ought to see her apartment."

Now Marie-Christine had a hand in Annie's pocket. "I love your drink," she said, picking it up.

"Oomph," said Annie as the hand moved suddenly deeper. She seemed completely used to such intimate public touching. Her eyes lovingly watched Marie-Christine pull an orange slice from the Lavender Julie with her tongue and proceed to eat it as suggestively as possible. Heads close together, they both broke into giggles. "God, I love you," said Annie.

And Sally could see why.

"Orange," Marie-Christine called to Liz as she came near them.

Sally started to reach for another orange slice.

"Orange tablecloths," Marie-Christine said. Sally surreptitiously put Marie-Christine's orange slice away. Was she really so captivated by Liz's old lover?

"And yellow wrought-iron chairs. And little lavender flower vases with fresh flowers," said Marie-Christine. She turned those blue eyes on Sally. "You *are* planning a lavender awning?"

"Yes," Sally said hurriedly, as if trying to please her. "And we know a dyke florist. She brings the flowers we use now."

Annie's hand lay lovingly around the back of Marie-Christine's neck. Now and then Marie-Christine rubbed against it. Occasionally she looked at Annie's lips and licked her own. "Yes," she said, "the flowers brighten *Cafe Femmes* very much."

Liz bumped into Sally on her way to grab a bottle. Sally stopped her, hands on her soft upper arms. "I love you," she said, pulling Liz to her, holding her tightly, briefly.

Liz started to break away after the hug, then seemed to sense the urgency in Sally's body. She pressed against her, offering those soft lips, speaking with those sultry eyes. Sally remembered every reason she'd fallen for Liz in the first place as she saw her through Marie-Christine's eyes, younger and in Paris. It was a long kiss, and they had a lot of orders to catch up on afterwards, but, Sally thought, watching Annie Heaphy and Marie-Christine cavorting at the pinball machine, it was the season.

*   *   *   *   *

And still later, in their own bed, Liz was saying, "God, you're good," her voice deep and velvety with satisfaction as she pulled Sally to her. In the dim glow of dawn both their mouths shone slick with each other's juices.

"Better than Marie-Christine?" Sally asked. She hadn't planned to, but she was all too aware that their excitement had been more intense than usual.

"Hmm," Liz said, as if comparing them.

"Liz?" asked Sally nervously.

Liz laughed, sliding her wet mouth back and forth against Sally's. "Better than Marie-Christine," she said firmly, just before her tongue touched Sally's lips. "Sal," she whispered, her voice as tense as her thighs against her lover.

Sally held Liz tightly with one arm while the other moved down. The second time, with Liz moving and moving against her fingers, Liz came just as fast as the first. Then Liz drifted off to sleep in her arms.

But Sally couldn't sleep. Though she knew she'd have to get up in a few hours to open the bar, she was still too aroused by Liz, too excited by the night. Her mind was filled with pictures. She pulled Liz to her, kissed the soft greying hair. She remembered the warmth of their parting from Marie-Christine and Annie.

"I love you, love you," whispered Sally now into Liz's hair. Liz stirred, groaned sensuously, pressed her hot, now loose, thighs against Sally. Should she wake her for more lovemaking?

"Umm," Liz moaned.

Sally found she was hugging her as she had hugged Marie-Christine at parting. It was an entirely different sensation without clothes. She gasped to feel Liz's hand between her legs, to realize Liz had come very wide awake.

Liz moaned again. "How ready you are," she whispered into Sally's ear.

Sally felt Liz's hand slide easily on her, inside her. And she remembered, just before she gave herself completely over to sensation, how many hours her long slow fuse had been burning. How near the explosion it must be.

At the window, the sun's progress matched Sally's. By the time she cried out finally, loudly, it filled the window. Sunday would not be dim.

AT A BAR IX:
HALLOWEEN

The two little trees the Neighborhood Association had planted outside *Cafe Femmes* were all decked out in reds and browns, greens and yellows. When the breezes stirred their leaves they waved and fluttered till tall blonde Sally the Bartender laughed at the thought that they *might* just be flirting with each other. They reminded her of so many of the kids coming into the bar in bright boisterous colors, preening in search of a mate. She'd gone all through that with Liz, and now they were like denuded winter trees with each other, down to their bare graceful shapes, lovingly familiar and polished by caresses.

"Boy oh boy!" said Gabby, jangling the cowbells behind

the door as she burst in to make lunches for *Cafe Femmes'* new sidewalk restaurant. The light outside was as bright as the trees, but the bar, nestled between warehouses, didn't get much sun this time of day in the fall. "What a difference those trees make out there," said Gabby. "You can tell what season it is, even in Soho!"

Sally laughed again and wiped down the bar. The lunch crowds would start soon; Gabby's to sit at the sidewalk cafe and munch fancy sandwiches of cheese and avocado, watercress and anchovy; her own, with their take-out pizzas from up the street and their pitchers of beer. Gabby was slicing and singing already as she made preparations. Sally laughed once more, but to herself. Gabby had taken to wearing bright-colored overalls at work, with contrasting shirts. Today she wore loud gold overalls with a red shirt. She'd changed her hair recently too, letting the bangs grow out and sweeping them back. The grey it revealed added character to that cheerful, round-cheeked face.

"You figure out your costume yet?" called Gabby. Halloween was fast approaching and *Cafe Femmes* always held a contest.

Sally was installing a new washer on the faucet. "How about a bum?"

Gabby groaned. "You came as a bum last year."

"Then what did I do *two* years ago? I'll be that again."

"Robin Hood? In that dumb green mechanic's jump-suit?"

"And the pointy green hat with the feather," she protested, giving a last twist with the wrench. "What was wrong with that?"

"It didn't make it, Sal," Gabby said in a disparaging tone. "You looked like you stepped out of Jack and the Beanstalk."

"Humph," she said. She'd thought she looked really good. "What do you suggest?"

"I thought you'd never ask," said Gabby, striding to the bar. "Let me have my wake-up Julie."

She felt Gabby's eyes watch every move as she assembled the grape juice, seltzer, orange slice, lime and cherry that went into the Lavender Julie, a drink Sally had devised to keep Gabby on the wagon. "So?" she asked, adding a second cherry and handing it to her.

"You forgot the *straw* today. I don't know, Sal. You always forget something. Cheers."

Sally lifted her bottle of Perrier.

"Dee was telling me, this woman is renting the shop over her magic store. She thinks she might be a dyke."

"What's that got to do with the price of tea in China?" Gabby sipped noisily. "It's a *costume* shop." She paused as if for dramatic effect. "I was thinking, where she's a dyke and all, maybe you and Liz ought to invest a little of the profits in dressing your staff right for Halloween. You know, there's going to be a neighborhood association prize for the best-dressed business this year."

The cowbells chimed and six women entered bearing pizzas, speaking Spanish. One called, in English, "You want some, Sal?"

"Never touch the stuff before noon," she replied.

"Come on, Gabby. We don't even have to ask you."

Gabby headed for the pizza, but stopped and turned back to Sally. "What about it, Sal, want me to check out this costume shop?"

"Let me talk to Liz." She pushed two Cokes and a pitcher of beer toward a factory worker, then waved to three middle-aged women in pantsuits who'd settled at an outside table. The day had begun at *Cafe Femmes*.

* * * * *

On her next Monday off, the one day of the week *Cafe*

Femmes was closed, Sally agreed to go with Gabby to Dee's Magic World, and then upstairs to the costume shop. Normally, she spent Mondays with Liz, but once a month she liked being footloose and fancy-free in the big city—as long as she had Liz to go home to at night.

She stood on the Avenue of the Americas. There were a few bright trees in sight, leaves fluttering beside the international flags which furled and unfurled in the crisp fall breezes. The leaves and flags went limp all at once and the air felt warmer; she closed her eyes a moment to bask in the sun.

When she opened them, Gabby was in sight, sauntering toward her in red denim overalls, hands in her pockets. They set off toward Dee's on a side street just below the Village.

A block further on, Gabby looked at Sally; smells of fresh bread and French pastries stopped them in their tracks. Sally nodded. Just the right kind of day to munch on sweets as they walked through the sunlight. But then they thought they should bring something for Dee, something for Dee to take Willa, maybe something for the new lesbian at the costume shop.

"If she *is* one," said Gabby, whispering before the glass counter of baked goods.

"Even if she isn't," Sally suggested.

So they arrived in high, if glutted, spirits at Dee's Magic World carrying two bags each, one of cookies, two of pastries, another of *petits fours,* which they had almost emptied.

Sally jumped, as she did every time, at the wild maniacal laughter that greeted their entry. Gabby clapped her hands in glee, saying, "Just like Coney Island when I was growing up!" She shut and opened the door to trigger the laugh again.

In the small shadowy shop Gabby and Dee jokingly threatened to replace *Cafe Femmes'* cowbells with the laugh.

The walls were covered with foil and its folds and crinkles reflected all the different colored lights Dee had placed on counters and shelves. She didn't use the overhead lighting at all.

"So is the girl upstairs gay?" Gabby asked.

"As gay as they get. She's been over to dinner," Dee answered. Her long red hair glowed against her white shirt.

"Couples night?" asked Gabby casually.

Dee raised her red eyebrows. "As a matter of fact—" she teased.

"I figured. She's taken too."

"Uh-uh," Dee said, grinning mischievously, shaking her head so that the long hair brushed back and forth against her shoulders. "She's very single and lonely. You want the whole story before you go up?"

"You bet," said Gabby.

"She was living in Vermont, some hippie colony. Making costumes for a small-time local theater company. She moved back here because her grandmother's going blind and she wanted to help keep her out of a nursing home."

"A hippie?" Gabby asked.

"An ex-hippie."

"What's her name?"

"Amaretto."

"*What?*"

"She can't help it. Her mother worked for one of the hoity-toity shops here, buying hats. Rubbed elbows with the rich. Thought a classy name would snare her kid a classy guy."

"No wonder she turned into a hippie," muttered Gabby.

Sally picked up a stack of wooden blocks attached by two strips of fabric. "*I* remember these," she said, lifting and flipping them so that the blocks fell and turned without leaving the length of fabric. "*My* grandma gave me a set."

"Amaretto's grandmother—she likes to be called Nanny—

is cute as a button. She supported herself and Chandler, Amaretto's mother, making hats."

"Chandler," scoffed Gabby. "They run in the family, those crazy names."

"Nanny named her after her lover at the time."

Still flipping the blocks, Sally raised her eyebrows. Who ever heard of a grandma with a lover?

But Gabby had broken into a wide grin. "I'm in love," she announced.

"Amaretto's upstairs, waiting for Princess Charming," said Dee.

"Amaretto! It's Nanny *I* want," Gabby replied, bustling to the door. "Cute as a button—that's what you said, right? Had lovers even back then? Supported herself? Come on, Sal. I've got to get an introduction to this woman."

* * * * *

The steps to Amaretto's Costume Shop were narrow, and at one point right-angled, giving the effect of a winding staircase. Sally couldn't help thinking, after Dee's comment about Princess Charming, of the Castle where Sleeping Beauty lay. She felt a little shiver of excitement for Gabby. Maybe Gabby would end up with a Grandma-in-law.

"I thought she was on the *second* floor," said Gabby, huffing.

"Stop acting like a forty-year-old."

"I *am* a forty-year-old."

The shop was in the loft and was at least three times the size of Dee's Magic World, but stuffed with rack after rack of costumes. Light from large windows along one wall fell in wide swaths across the reds, the blue-greens, the golds and blacks and purples. The floor had been stripped down to a blond wood and highly polished. One wall was all mirrors, framed by dressing room lights. Facing the mirrors stood a slight woman in a white princess gown, sleeves puffed, skirt billowing.

"I'll be right with you," she called, making some additional adjustments to the costume.

"Like a bride," said Gabby in a hushed voice.

Sally looked at Gabby from the corner of her eye and smiled with satisfaction.

The woman twirled toward them, the air currents from her gown setting in motion several ceiling-hung mobiles alive with shining stars.

"Can I help you?" The voice was unexpectedly husky.

Sally waited for Gabby to explain their purpose, their friendship with Dee; but she just stood there, staring. Amaretto's hair was as long as Dee's, but all salt and pepper against an almost unlined face. She wore wire-rimmed glasses, half-tinted blue. She wasn't exactly beautiful, but she was striking. In the gown she looked regal.

The silence continued. Sally looked at her friend. Gabby responded by opening her mouth. "Uh," she said.

Sally took over.

Amaretto welcomed them, gave them herbal tea. Sally set hers aside, hoping Amaretto wouldn't notice. Gabby drank hers as if it were nectar.

She saw the costumes she wanted for herself and Liz immediately. Amaretto folded and pinned till Sally's fitted nicely. Liz would have to come in for a fitting as well.

"And you," said Amaretto, turning to Gabby. "You're so quiet and shy, we'll have to dress you in something dashing."

Gabby squared her shoulders. "Have you ever been to *Cafe Femmes?*" she asked, her voice small and dry-sounding. When Amaretto shook her head no, Gabby cleared her throat and went on, "*I* run the restaurant." Her normal boastfulness was tempered by her downcast, modest demeanor and a blush. But she looked quickly up, as if to see if Amaretto had been impressed by her announcement.

Amaretto seemed to be waiting for more.

"So I need something I can wear during the day, when the straight people are around. And then something at night, more, you know, more like—"

"Dykey?" Amaretto supplied.

"Two costumes?" asked Sally, who had agreed to pay.

"Maybe just one," Gabby conceded, "that could be added to."

Amaretto looked Gabby up and down with a professional eye. "A sailor," she concluded. "Even little girls wear sailor suits. I could put you in a middy blouse during the day, and a full dress uniform at night. I think you'd look quite handsome in both."

"You *do?*" asked Gabby, astonishment in her voice. She'd often complained that her chunky body wasn't capable of handsomeness.

The phone rang just then, and Gabby pulled a comb from her pocket while Amaretto's back was turned. But the comb never reached her hair.

"Nanny?" Amaretto shouted into the phone. "Nanny, what's wrong?"

But apparently there was no answer. She hung up and looked desperately around her. "My grandmother—I need to get over there fast."

Gabby, no longer the blushing suitor, whipped her comb back into her pocket. "Do what you need to to close up. I'll get a cab." As she dialed her eyes followed Amaretto, her shyness, her flustered manner gone. Sally had seen her like this before, especially helping to get rid of troublemakers at the bar. "Can I come with you?" Gabby asked Amaretto.

"What?" the distracted shop owner responded. "Of course. I may need help."

At the door downstairs, Gabby turned to Sally. "You

get stuff from Dee to make a sign that Amaretto's is closed for an emergency. I'll see you later."

Sally stood silently on the sidewalk, confused. Usually she was the one who told Gabby what to do. She watched as Amaretto took Gabby's hand and squeezed it. Gabby put a comforting arm across her shoulder and patted it. Then the cab pulled up and they were gone.

* * * * *

It was Halloween night. Often, in the two weeks since their trip to get costumes, Sally would stand absently, wiping the bar with a rag, remembering the two shops. Dee's, with its mystery and air of good magic; Amaretto's, with its enchantment and color. She had wanted to transform *Cafe Femmes* for Halloween, to give it all those same qualities.

"The crazy laugh!" Gabby had suggested. And Dee had offered to rent her a tape for the day.

She'd accepted, but that wasn't quite what she was after. . . .

By the time the Neighborhood Association judges had arrived that noon, the tape was just background to lights covered by orange Japanese lanterns, and ceiling of foil that reflected the orange, and a window painted by Pam, a local artist who came into the bar for dykes, not sandwiches. Often, she'd sit in a corner sketching. She'd decided to turn the plate glass window into a ballroom, and women who might have frequented lesbian bars in 1920s Paris now danced across it in long black skirts, half-masks held to their faces. It all looked good, but Sally knew *Cafe Femmes* wouldn't win the Neighborhood contest.

How could Halloween decorations be judged in daylight? Only now, at night when the costumed lesbians and a few gay men making the rounds were crowding the bar, did the decorations look complete. The crazy laughter interrupted Anne Murray, Barry Manilow, Linda Ronstadt, at just the right times. The real dancers jounced and swayed before the window mural. Night shadows deepened between the glowing lanterns. It was still *Cafe Femmes*, but certainly everyone was transformed. Sally, like Gabby, had gone home to dress, but was already back behind the bar serving drinks in her samurai costume beside Liz the geisha.

"You guys look great!" shouted Gabby, the crazy laughter announcing her entrance.

Sally lifted one of her two swords in salute and Gabby saluted back in a white uniform of vaguely naval design, including the white, stiff-brimmed cap. Liz winked at Sally on her way to deliver a drink. They'd both noticed that Gabby had found shiny black elevator shoes; she was just as tall as Amaretto who stood beside her in that same white princess gown she'd worn at her shop. They looked like radiant angels in their whites. Holding hands, they seemed immensely pleased with themselves and each other.

Gabby let go of Amaretto's hand, moved quickly to a short elderly woman who had come in with them. "Nanny," Gabby proudly introduced her. Nanny wore a red sequined dress, a wide-brimmed feathered hat, and a harlot's bright makeup.

"What," Sally asked the older woman admiringly, "are you dressed as?"

Nanny thrust her chin up. "A whorehouse madam," she said firmly. Her voice had the same huskiness as Amaretto's. "I always wished I could be one for a day. When Amaretto gave me the run of her shop this afternoon, I thought, now's my chance!"

Chuckling at both Nanny and Gabby, Sally replenished someone's beer glass, made change. Gabby must have been planning this entrance every minute of the last two weeks. She hadn't said another word about Amaretto, except to mention that Nanny's emergency had been a false alarm; her fall had resulted in a bruised hip, but no broken bones.

"A bar?" Nanny was saying when Sally returned to the group. "This feels like a party, not a bar." Nanny saw in shadows only.

"I'll go get someone to give up their table for us," Gabby announced, a little self-importantly, fitting her officer's cap more tightly to her head.

"Don't you do any such thing, young woman," Nanny said. Gabby stopped in her tracks, tiptoed back beside Nanny as if pretending she'd never left. "I've been sitting at bars all my life. It'll be good to get on a stool again."

Sally smiled. The love that shone from Gabby's eyes onto that old woman! And into Amaretto's, when their eyes met over Nanny's head.

"And how long has this been going on?" Liz inquired in an amused voice, grinning at Gabby.

"Gabby wanted to surprise you," Amaretto explained in that low voice. "The shop was already closed the day we went over to Nanny's, and it seemed silly to go back to work. Gabby, once the emergency was over, turned out to be so much fun! We visited with Nanny for a while, then went over to Gabby's and drank Lavender Julies all afternoon while we talked." She looked at Gabby. "She made me laugh more than I had in years. And I'd seen her other side, too, when she'd done exactly what I'd needed her to without stepping on my toes." Amaretto tossed back her greying hair and laughed. "In those funny, funny red overalls."

Sally brought them a round of Julies, all except for Nanny, who insisted on a "highball." When, Sally wondered, *had* she last seen Gabby in her red overalls, or the gold ones, or her turquoise painters' pants? The flagrant colors had fallen just as they were falling from those little trees out front, from trees all over the city.

"To your little bar," toasted Nanny, lifting her highball

toward what must have been a shadowy Liz and Sally. Sally wondered if Nanny's very lack of sight injected just the notes of mystery and enchantment she'd tried to achieve in decorating the bar. Nanny went on, "And to lovers, finding each other, everywhere!"

THE SWASHBUCKLER,* AFTERWARD:
THE EASTER FEAST

The sun once danced for joy on warm Easter mornings. Frenchy remembered waking at dawn, filled with excitement. For days ahead all the little girls on her block had readied their pastels, their navy blues, their patent leather shoes. Frenchy, thrilled by the holiday vibrations in the air, would be anxious to stay outside playing and anxious, at the same time, to be alone again with her Easter basket of fancy-colored foils nestled in green cellophane grasses.

This was her thirtieth Easter, and somewhere along the line the holiday's suns had weakened. dimmed to what she

---

*A novel by the author, published 1985.

could see today through the dirty subway window. She and Mercedes were crossing the East River on their way to Jessie and Mary's home in College Point. The water was grey and lumpy-looking, with none of the sparkle a full sun could give it. There had been no little girls showing off in the Queens neighborhoods the train passed over—the day was too cold. The neighborhoods themselves had been lifeless, wan, as if exhausted by winter.

Frenchy longed for the sun today. For the return of those feelings of giddy excitement that swept her past her worries. She needed badly to shake her feeling of depression, but she couldn't quite name what was bothering her. She reached for Mercedes' hand as they left the subway.

"Hey, lover, welcome back."

"I was thinking," said Frenchy, still dreamy.

They saw their bus and sprinted for it.

"Cold as hell," said Mercedes, shuddering as she pressed up close to Frenchy on the rear seat.

"That's what you get for dressing like some college kid," Frenchy teased, surveying Mercedes' button-down collar, burgundy crew neck and corduroy jacket. Her own new charcoal suit and black turtleneck felt more substantial, especially with the long red silk scarf Mercedes had given her.

Mercedes grinned mischievously. "And how about you?" she teased back. "Butches don't get cold, right?"

Frenchy combed back her black hair expertly. "Right," she said. "I guess that makes *you* femme."

"Listen, see if *I* sleep without pajamas tonight!" Mercedes threatened.

"*I* never met pajamas *I* couldn't get past."

They jostled each other affectionately, then sat comfortably in silence, holding hands. The sun broke through the clouds, and on every street corner they passed, little kids crept cautiously into the brightness as if testing cold water. By the time they walked the remaining blocks to Jessie and Mary's, they had to wind their way through little girls skipping rope. Frenchy laughed out loud for joy at the sight of them like blossoming flowers all over the city streets.

But then she remembered the night before and, as they waited for their friends to open the door, the grey clouds descended even lower over her head.

Her impulse was to take Mercedes' hand again, to hold on tight until the comfort of that touch drove away the sick feeling in her stomach.

Last night had been perfect for lovemaking. They were rested, in fine moods, had had dinner by candlelight. Mercedes turned her on as much as ever. But after she'd made love to Mercedes and Mercedes had turned to her, she'd started to worry again. It wasn't that she didn't like what Mercedes did, or how she did it. As always, it was wonderful. But again last night, after what seemed like hours of frustrating attempts to let herself have an orgasm, after getting so close and losing it, after clearing her head time after time only to have some disruptive thought invade it, Frenchy had pretended, again, to come. She couldn't disappoint Mercedes that way. And she couldn't explain what had gone wrong if she'd wanted to.

To stop coming with a lover—what did it mean? With Pam, orgasm had been simple, she'd taken it for granted. But Pam hadn't been anywhere near as important as Mercedes. And with Mercedes she'd had no problems at all. But now, when it was becoming plainer and plainer that they would be together forever, Frenchy could no longer give herself to their lovemaking. And she wanted to so badly. . . .

The door swung open. "Hey, guys! Boy, it's good to see you again." Jessie threw her arms around both of them at once and talked behind them all the way up the stairs, as if the force of her words could make the climb easier.

Jessie lived with Mary on the third floor of a big old brown house owned by Mary's parents. On the first two floors lived Mary's sisters with their families.

Mary wore a ruffled apron, blue eye shadow and gold rings. "You met Mario's wife Lisa before, didn't you?" she asked. Mario was her brother, the cop. The rest of the family had all gone to Disneyworld for Easter.

"Eat!" said Mary, and with a sweeping gesture set a tray of crisply brown turnover-like pastries on the coffee table. Lisa, a tiny woman with soft brown hair and a sweet smile, picked up one and offered it to Frenchy. She bit into it and was surprised by the smooth and soft spinach and cheese filling, rich with garlic.

"What're you drinking, guys?" asked Jessie. Then, too excited to wait for them to notice, she exclaimed, "How do you like my new bar, Frenchy?"

The spinach pastry had made her aware of a queasiness in her stomach somewhere between excitement at having Easter dinner with her oldest pal and anxiety about her sex life with Mercedes. She left the others to join Jessie. "It's very sharp," she commented.

"You don't sound impressed," said Jessie with a frown. "Remember when we had to go to the Village to get a drink? Wait in line to use the bathroom?" Rearranging cut glass decanters on the swing-out counter, she boasted, "This is the life, Frenchy."

The furniture, Frenchy noticed, was still shrouded in its stiff plastic protective covers just as it had been several years before when she'd first seen it. "I am impressed," she said. "Your own bar. Jess, you've come up in the world."

Now Jessie could be modest. "Nah, this was only to celebrate getting my promotion to foreman."

"Congratulations! I'll drink to that."

They clinked glasses and went across the room to the rest of the group.

Mercedes smiled the way she always did when she was about to tell Frenchy how much she loved her. The twinge returned to Frenchy's gut. What would she think if she knew about Frenchy faking it? Would she still love her? How could she when Frenchy was lying to her?

Without knocking, Mario entered the apartment. "Sorry I'm late," he said as he strode, short and hairy and barrelchested, straight to the bar.

"Help yourself," Jessie said unnecessarily.

Only when he'd mixed and taken the first swallow of his scotch and water did Mario turn to his wife. "Hi, Chickadee!" he said, lifting her clear off the floor in a hug.

Mary laughed. "How come you never do that to me?" she asked Jessie.

Mario poked Jessie. " 'Cause you don't work out at the gym every day, right Jess?"

"Mario," Jessie said in response, "this is Mercedes and Frenchy."

Frenchy solemnly shook his hand. "Glad to meet you." She wasn't at all certain she was. Cops busted gays. What was she doing having Easter dinner with one? At least he wasn't in uniform. She wandered to the window, pulled away by her desperation. Was it easier, being straight? No, they had their problems too, but when she felt like this it was hard not to fall into thinking maybe the world was right, maybe being gay was going against too much, making things too much harder. Not that she had a choice—or wanted to. Easter day clouds wafted across the sky like puffs of spring to come.

"Frenchy—you okay?" Mercedes had joined her.

"Of course. Why wouldn't I be?"

Mercedes narrowed her eyes. "I don't know. But ever since last night—"

A feeling of panic clenched her insides shut like a fist. When Mercedes left to join Mario on the couch, Frenchy refilled her glass. What was she doing to their love, she worried. Now Mercedes was thinking she'd upset her. She strode to her window again. All the little girls in pastels and navy blues were jumping rope, wheeling doll carriages with Easter bunnies for babies. Their brothers were in the street whacking a wooden puck with sticks. Their play, their impassioned yells, absorbed Frenchy. When she turned back to the room she was calmer. Smells seemed to storm out of the kitchen, intent on overwhelming everyone. Frenchy had worried that she wouldn't be able to eat because she was too upset, but now her mouth was watering.

Mercedes was saying, "Mario's beat is out at Queens College, where Lydia wants to study." Lydia, Mercedes' daughter, was spending this Easter back in Harlem, with her grandmother.

Frenchy laughed. "At least we know she'll be safe!"

Mario, after his fast start, was drinking Seven-Up. "I always need something to relax me when I get home," he said, then winked. "Being as how we're in company today I thought a drink would be quicker than a long cuddle with Lisa."

Again, Frenchy was drawn out of herself enough to laugh. "That's what I love after a long day at the A&P."

"A cuddle with Lisa?" asked Mercedes, teasing.

"With you," Frenchy replied softly, lovingly.

"What do you do?" asked Lisa.

"With Frenchy?" teased Mercedes again.

"Head *cashier*," Frenchy answered, winking toward Mercedes.

Mario said, "That's a rough job. I used to clerk at Grand Union. You get all the crazies who think they've been gyped out of a buck."

It wasn't often that Frenchy found somone who knew to be impressed by her job. She sat up straighter. "I'd rather do that than walk a beat. I'd be scared to death," she offered, starting to like Mario despite herself.

"Ride," corrected Mario. "Me and my partner ride around Queens. But that's not always safe either. The other day this drunk rammed into us at an intersection. My partner's wearing one of those whiplash collars."

Mercedes said, "I saw more of that kind of injury at the hospital this winter. . . ." She shook her head. "It was all the ice that did it."

"Are you a nurse?" asked Lisa.

"Nuclear technician," Mercedes answered.

"Even *your* job isn't safe," said Mario. "You could be exposed to that radiation they're curing people with."

Lisa sneaked up behind Mario and hugged him. His face lighting with pleasure, he said, "This one insists on working too, even though I offered to pay her to stay home and look pretty for me."

"I love kids too much," Lisa said, laughing. She explained, "I work in the Headstart Program."

"When you have a batch of your own . . ." Frenchy said.

Mercedes' hand shot to Frenchy's knee, as if to stop her.

Frenchy looked at her, not understanding.

"That's okay," Mario said. "We're past hiding it or beating ourselves with wet pasta over it." Lisa slipped around and sat next to him. "We can't *have* kids. My fault. I was born broken." He laughed and put his arm around Lisa. "When the doctor told me, I was so ashamed I couldn't even tell Lisa for a month. It got so bad I wouldn't look her in the eye."

"Then," said Lisa, putting her arm as far around Mario's waist as it would reach, "Mario told me. I was so relieved he hadn't been planning to leave me—which is what I thought by then—that I realized he was much more important to me than babies."

"But we're still talking about adopting." He drew Lisa tighter against himself, kissing her gently on the forehead. "Most important, we've been closer than ever since I broke down and spilled the beans. I get scared every time I think about what I could have done to us holding out on her like that."

"Chow time!" Jessie cried, bearing a steaming, sweet-smelling ham glossy with glaze, decorated by slices of pineapples. Behind her came Mary with lasagne, deep red and spicy-smelling.

The flat was hot with oven-heated, sweet-smelling cooking fumes. While everyone stood around waiting for Jessie to carve the ham, Frenchy wandered once more to the window.

The block was nearly empty of children now; they were inside, just like her, waiting to be served a holiday feast. She felt unutterably lonely as she looked down at the deserted street, felt separate from her friends. Only an elderly woman in a long black coat and kerchief, hauling a shopping cart, moved under the cloud-covered sky. Why wasn't she with people of her own? Did she know there was a holiday going on in the world? Did she feel as alone as Frenchy?

Maybe, Frenchy worried, she didn't have anyone. Maybe, and she felt as if she were falling into a bottomless pit, maybe she was a lesbian who had ended up, as the straight world warned, alone and destitute in her old age. Frenchy found herself imagining how the woman had lost her last lover by holding back some important part of herself. Mario had faced up to the truth. Had Frenchy spent too many years lying to one-night stands, faking about herself to keep her freedom, living the gay life to its hilt—was it too late for her to learn to be honest?

Mercedes caught her with tears in her eyes. "What's going on, Frenchy? We've been calling you to the table. You catch my crazies? Or are you just getting your period?"

As a matter of fact, thank goodness, she was due for her period. Mercedes held her for a moment, and Frenchy wanted to stay safe, safe in those arms forever. "I guess it's just my pre-period blues. . . ."

Mercedes led her to the table which was now a forest of dishes.

Mary held up two golden-brown loaves of bread braided around hard-boiled eggs still in their shells. "These," Mary said proudly, "are my first Easter breads."

"Do you eat them?" asked Frenchy.

"If you have an Italian wife," Jessie said with a laugh, "you eat everything on the table or she feels hurt!" There was an edge to her laugh.

Mary said, as if defending herself, "Or if you're an Italian kid! Mamma used to get so hurt over Mario's picky eating."

"And," Mario said laughing, "neither of us married Italian girls!"

"Remember what Pop said about not marrying an Italian?" Mary offered this in a tone that suggested this was a traditional holiday joke. "He said, 'No wonder you can't have no kids!' "

Mario laughed as if on cue. "Did he ever shit when I told him it was my fault. Then Mamma says—"

Jessie supplied the punch line: "You never did eat right!"

In the midst of the laughter Mary again yelled, "Eat!" and they began.

But Frenchy's attention had wandered. *Why?* Her troubled brain went on and on even as she ate, even as she joked and made conversation. Why had she begun having this trouble? She had wanted Mercedes more than anything on earth. Back when she'd first fallen for her, and she'd thought they couldn't be lovers because they were both butch, at least she had known what was wrong, it was simple. Then later when she'd come on to Mercedes, gambling that she'd turn femme, she'd still known why it wouldn't work, understood Mercedes' rejection.

Everyone was laughing. Mercedes had just realized, her mouth full of fried peppers, that they were hot. "Holy shit!" she yelled when she could.

"Some hot-blooded Latin you are!" Jessie's face, after a second helping, was red and shiny with sweat. She unbuttoned her cream-colored pants. She'd discarded her matching jacket while carving. "Ohhh," she groaned when the main course was over, "I ate too much."

Mario laughed. "You always say that, Jess. Why don't you just stop when you're full?"

"You leave Jessie alone," Mary said, like some stern grandmotherly figure. "What's wrong with a healthy appetite?"

"Healthy! She's getting fat," Mario said, still laughing. "She's proving her love just the way I wouldn't to Mamma. And the way you did." He flung a cork coaster, frisbee-like, toward his sister. "The first thing I remember in school, some kid comes up to me and says, 'It's the fat girl's brother! Whatsamatter, Bones, she eat all yours?' I slaughtered him."

"I never heard another remark about my weight," Mary said proudly.

Jessie looked earnestly toward Mary. "Is that why you like to see me eat? So you'll know I love you?"

"Don't be silly," snapped Mary, rising to clear the table.

Jessie's patter thinned, but revived with praise when Mary triumphantly appeared with Italian pastries. "From Giamoni's Bakery. The best!"

Lisa and Mary moved to the kitchen to do dishes. The others went to the living room to somnolently watch a football game on TV.

Mercedes was stretched out on the couch, her head in Frenchy's lap. Frenchy gently, almost reverently, stroked her dark short hair, her soft dark skin. She could see night beginning to seep into the sky through her window across the room. It was still light enough, though, for the little kids to be out again after dinner, running and dirtying their clothing with abandon; she could hear their shouts. Her depression was lifting. Here was Mercedes, safe on her lap, still her lover, her companion, all that she'd ever wanted in a woman.

And here around them, immobilized by their holiday feast and the movement of the small, brightly-colored figures on the screen, were people just like them, with their own troubles.

Frenchy focused her thoughts on Lisa and Mario. They couldn't have kids, but went on anyway, maybe loving each other better because of the trouble they'd been through. And Jessie, and Mary—for years they'd been having some kind of problem about food. Every couple, it seemed, had its test to take, maybe lots of them, before passing from being in love to loving for good.

What made her think she was so special, that she could fix this problem all by herself? How dumb could she get, assuming Mercedes would split because something was wrong.

Mercedes was stirring on her lap. Frenchy held tight to her. When had she last felt so safe and loved? When she was her mother's little girl in pastels, playing in the sunny streets. What had she done to lose the joy, the love, besides grow up and choose colors different from her mother's? She smiled. She wasn't going to lose *this* woman's love.

Mercedes squeezed her leg affectionately and got up to go to the bathroom. Frenchy admired her butchy walk, her womanly body. She rose and crossed the room again, and opened her window wide, felt bathed in the cool, fresh-smelling air. Mary and Lisa talked behind her, Jessie and Mario still watched the game. "That air feels good!" cried Jessie. The kids outside were one by one answering their mothers' calls and fleeing the gathering dark for their well-lighted homes.

Why was she resurrecting all the old hurt of her mother's rejection? Why was she expecting Mercedes to turn on her? Mercedes hadn't fallen for the child in pastels, but for the woman she'd become.

Mercedes joined her at the window again. Frenchy turned toward her. "I love you," she said, with a smile that came freely and felt good.

"Hey," Mercedes kidded, "here's my girlfriend back again!"

The sun was setting, but it would dance again tomorrow. And she would begin talking to Mercedes on the bus going home.

BABE AND EVIE II:
THANKSGIVING

It was Thanksgiving Eve Day, but the Christmas cactuses were blooming blithely in the hothouse, each new color like an early gift.

"What are we going to do with you?" scolded Evie in a gruff, but loving voice. She leaned over them, at fifty-five her big-boned body looking soft even through the green one-piece uniform.

"Has this jungle got you talking to yourself, or did you and Babe finally put some money in the bank?" asked Freddy, her favorite groundskeeper. He stood at the open back door in a green uniform identical to hers, and looking like an aging muscular altar boy, bearing a shovel instead of a cross. Cold air stirred the moist heat of the hothouse in the Botanical Gardens.

She ran a hand in aggravation through her grizzled grey hair. Every year the Parks Department held a Christmas flower display and the cactuses were the highlight. "They're enough to make up my mind to retire right now." She looked down at them and mumbled, "And I would if I didn't think giving in to my dream would make Babe miserable."

"Aren't they gorgeous," said Freddy, closing the door and coming in closer to peer at them. He was too vain to wear his glasses.

"Out!" Evie cried, making shooing motions. "Every time you come in here trailing that equipment you knock one of these poor babies over." She picked up her clippers and began to snap at begonia stems.

Freddy had scuttled back to the doorway. "Babe doesn't want you to retire?" he asked, as if to take the attention away from himself.

She thought for a moment. "You know Babe. Mum's the word. But I know she wants to travel. And if I retire we won't be able to afford to. Babe's always said I should wait right up to sixty-five to get my full benefits. But if I don't retire, who knows if I'll even be here in ten years to finally open my little repair shop up on the Avenue?"

"When's your notice due to the City?"

"If I want to get out at twenty-five years, they'll need it Friday."

Freddy shook his head in wonder. "Wow. Two days from handing in your retirement. When I'm fifty-five, I'll only have...." He concentrated, and ticked off years on his fingers. "If I started here when I was thirty-one, and I'm forty-six now—"

"Fifteen years," Evie calculated for him.

"Okay, fifteen. So I'll have to work till I'm...." He paused again, but this time just waited.

"Fifty-six."

"Ten years more!"

Evie laughed. "Why don't you get Theodore to support you?" she joked.

He sighed. "Theodore says he's so much older than me, he'll die first. And I'm not likely to get widow's benefits." He stared dejectedly at a huge chrysanthemum.

She went to him and poked at his waist to tickle him. "Look chipper, boy, your turn will come."

He squirmed away, laughing helplessly. "Beast!" he managed to shout. Then, catching his breath, he said, "It's not retirement I'm worried about."

"Are the dachshunds sick again?" she asked, backing him around a table of plants, fingers at the ready.

Freddy shook his head and, up against a sink, said in a small voice, "You didn't want me to tell you the next time."

"Oh no," she said, throwing up her arms and stalking to the other end of the table. "Theodore's gone again, isn't he?"

Nodding, Freddy perched on a stool. He smelled like lime aftershave. His eyes, sad now, seemed even bluer, and younger, more innocent and trusting. "What'll I do if he's not home by Thanksgiving?"

She slammed her clippers on the wooden table, not caring that Freddy jumped. "I don't know *why* you put up with that man. You'd think he was a goddamned movie star, not some white-haired beanpole of a City employee."

"He's a good man," Freddy said in gentle defense. "A fine man. He's bold in his dreams."

"And you're a fine good man who deserves his boyfriend's respect."

"Shh," Freddy said quickly, finger to his lips.

Evie grumbled, "Serve him right to have to support you for getting fired over being upset about him."

"If only I knew for sure whether this latest dream is a

new poem, or young and handsome. I haven't gotten any younger these past twenty-one years." He ran his hands down his still-slim hips.

Evie was spading soil into pots with a vengeance. *"Why* does he have to disappear for days on end to write a poem?"

"Epics," Freddy explained with a sigh, as if he'd been over this before. "He writes epics. Like Homer. You remember studying *The Odyssey* with Mrs. Schneider at the high school. They take a long time to write."

She glowered at a newly rooted plant as she readied its soil, remembering the first time she'd watched this happen, not long after she and Freddy, having worked together several years, met at a party and discovered their common sexuality. She had never suspected her impishly handsome young Irish Catholic co-worker of being gay. In fact, she'd imagined him to be one of those youngest Irish sons, not bright enough for the priesthood—one brother already a soldier, the other already a cop—who lived with his mother and prayed away impure thoughts. They'd been great friends ever since their revelations, occasionally double-dating, each couple careful to include the other at mixed parties.

"If he gave some young fella half a chance," said Freddy, "the kid would be crazy not to grab Theodore."

Evie liked Theodore, but her loyalty was to Freddy. "Personally, I don't think you have to worry for a minute. Theodore's sixty, for chrissake," she said, making room for the newly potted plant on the edge of a shelf of its elders.

His eyes and voice soft, Freddy said, "A distinguished-looking older man."

She stopped herself, resisting further criticism of Theodore. After all, Freddy probably couldn't imagine what she saw in her cute, curly-haired Babe, nor what Babe saw in her. "Here you go, Junior," she said, passing a fallen, slightly wilted flower to him. "Wear it in your lapel. Maybe someone will notice you and be your consolation."

"Yuk," said Freddy, a look of comic disdain on his face as he rose to return to his digging. "You know I can't *stand* other men. There's not another in this town who'd dance to Johnny Mathis with me."

It was so seldom Freddie acted camp that Evie had to smile.

"Do you think," he breathed, delicately fingering the flower with his strong, chapped hands, "we'll ever have one of our little dance evenings again, just the four of us and Johnny Mathis?"

"Get your lazy tail out of here," she scolded good-humoredly. "Of course we will. Johnny and Elvis and Mantovani's whole damn orchestra. You know Theodore'll be back. And to stay this time, if I have to retire just to keep my eye on him. *You* can go traveling with Babe."

"It's a deal," said Freddy, swinging his shovel to his shoulder. It struck the newly potted plant and pushed it crashing to the floor. He looked guiltily toward Evie, then ran for the door as she started toward him, clippers menacingly in hand.

* * * * *

At holidays, Evie's family had always massed in one another's homes, Evie's "roommate" Babe included. But then her parents, aunts, uncles, older cousins, had one by one begun to die, and her sisters and brothers now celebrated Thanksgiving at the homes of their children spread across the state and country. For the past several years it had been just Babe and her and the cats: Boots and Leonardo da Kitty, the latter named by Theodore. Evie savored their holiday rituals as much as the cats savored their special holiday treats.

"Hey, Babe!" she hollered up the steep outside stairs to their third-floor flat.

Babe, a smiling, sprightly figure with a grey permanent,

opened the back door and held the cats at bay while Evie struggled up with a bag of groceries and the wrapped turkey. Neither woman ever used the front entrance, or the front stairs. Something about all that oily-smelling polished wood intimidated them, it seemed, with their arms always full of laundry, or electrical supplies for Evie's little workshop, or Babe's sewing materials. Except for Evie's uniforms, Babe made all their clothes.

"Such a big turkey!" Babe said, eyes laughing as if anticipating Evie's joke.

"I'm no turkey!" Evie said in that gruff affectionate voice. She set her purchases on the yellow formica tabletop and turned to envelop Babe in a long hug punctuated by loud kisses. "Smells good in here already," she said after one last squeeze.

"Leftover casserole for supper. But I see I don't have to worry about menus for a while. You're planning on turkey soup, turkey casserole, turkey pot pie—turkey ice cream maybe?"

Evie laughed in the center of their orange and yellow kitchen. The cats had left their dinners and prowled now for affection. Evie picked both up at once and hugged them too. They leapt to the floor, indignant and disgruntled. She grew serious. "Theodore's taken off again. I got extra food in case you might like to have Freddy for dinner tomorrow."

"Stuffed or with an apple in his mouth?" Babe asked, winking. Then she, too, grew serious. "The poor little guy. Of course he should come to dinner. Tell him to come at two. I won't have him ordering the blue plate special over at the diner all by himself just because Theodore's put on his genius cap again."

Evie gave her another hug, loving her for her warmth, her caring, her immediate reply.

Babe handed Evie a clean tablecloth and gave her a gentle

push. "Set the table. This is ready to eat." She pulled the casserole from the oven.

After dinner Evie called Freddy. Babe was making stuffing and homemade cranberry sauce; Evie could hear her singing along with a radio station that played Peggy Lee, Glenn Miller, Julie London, and imagined her sipping sweet Manischewitz wine and waltzing with the celery, with bags of cranberries, throughout the evening.

The cooking smells were everywhere. She went to her shop to finish rewiring her second cousin Gertie's heirloom lamp, an ornate heavy thing the woman doted on. "If I decide to retire," she said aloud to it, "I could fix monsters like you full time." She looked askance at it, wondering if she'd ever repaired an uglier lamp. Even if no one came into her shop because she was a woman doing repairs, she'd have her pension to fall back on. On the other hand, how could she lose? Mr. Guadino was about to close up shop and move to Southern California. She'd grown up in the neighborhood, and family and friends all over would be customers.

Of course she'd miss working at the park, she pointed out to herself, laughing quietly. No more kids assaulting the souvenir booth she ran all summer over at the zoo, no more catching colds all winter going from the hothouse into the snow, no more dumb City politics. Just a neat roomy shop with a big window through which she could watch everything that went on in the neighborhood, and wave to everyone. She'd be her own boss, and Babe would do the books. Grateful customers would pour in, arms filled with lamps and radios and vacuum cleaners and fans.

She grew misty-eyed to think of not working with Freddy. She'd never worked with another gay person before. It somehow made up for a lot of years she'd spent lying to herself to co-workers, always feeling somehow in the wrong. And she'd miss the routine, the ease with which she could complete every task. Miss the holidays, the paid vacations.

Smiling, she pushed wire through the monster's base, and remembered her pride when they began to let her repair rowboats with Freddy, even though she was a woman. The next year they'd told her she could rewire the souvenir stand for the popcorn popper and hot dog machine. It had been one of her proudest moments when the City electrician had checked it out and found no faults. She glowed at the memory.

She stripped the end of a wire, thinking of Babe, of her yearning to travel. When they'd first talked of Evie's retirement—Babe's wouldn't come for several more years—they'd planned to take the difference between Evie's salary and the pension she would have received, and use this "extra" money to travel. They'd both accumulated months of vacation time. California, Nova Scotia, the Grand Canyon. . . . Evie was the only one in her family who'd never even been to Maine. But then she'd decided to open her shop, and now she was too anxious to wait till she was sixty-five. The excitement about *Evie's Electric* had eclipsed her own yen to travel for a while. It remained Babe's dream.

In bed long before Babe finished her holiday preparations in the kitchen, she dreamed of dining on a cruise ship off some tropical coast, relishing Babe's lush cranberry sauce and turkey stuffing.

At two AM she woke to the sound of Babe, wineglass in hand, passing through to the bathroom. She heard her brush her teeth, then saw her slip into the light blue silken nightgown she saved for special occasions. A pleasurable shudder moved down Evie's body as she watched Babe hurry to bed. This was her favorite part of their holiday eve tradition, begun way back when Babe had cooked their first Thanksgiving dinner.

She gave a low wolf-whistle at Babe in the glow of the dim nightlight and lifted the covers to welcome her into the warm bed. The startled cats fled. She felt Babe's cool hands slip immediately under the waistband of her pajamas, felt her fingers dig into the soft warm flesh around her waist. What faraway place would Babe conjure tonight for their lovemaking? A few nights ago it had been Spain, hot and brilliant white at siesta time. The week before an ice palace as in Dr. Zhivago. Evie's favorite was the Vermont trip in late spring, either a daytime interlude naked among the wildflowers, or the image of a heavy quilt and a brick-warmed bed in the cool nights. Travel was Babe's passion in more ways than one; if they couldn't yet indulge in the real thing, they didn't do without. She pulled Babe to her and squeezed her bottom with both hands.

"You smell like Manischewitz," she whispered as she slid the blue nightgown up. "And stuffin'."

She felt Babe push her cool body against her, silently, eagerly, as if she didn't want to play tonight. Babe took Evie's hand and pressed it against herself, so the fingers went in easily, slowly.

"Ohhhh," said Babe.

* * * * *

They rose late on Thanksgiving day, stretching and cuddling under the blue and white quilt Evie had gotten in a trade with a sister-in-law for assembling some Tiffany-style lamp kits. Once up, Babe immediately started cooking, and Evie tuned in the parade on TV. She stood in the middle of the living room laughing at the cartoon character floats; in her flannel pajamas and long velour robe, she marched into the bathroom to the music of an Oklahoma high school band.

By early afternoon everything that could be done was done, and Babe urged Evie to sit out on the back porch with her.

The air felt light and cool after their warm kitchen. The "porch" was a narrow wooden planking that connected the stairs to their door, and they'd strung three chairs along it facing out over the rail. Their view was of a vacant lot, in spring filled with chicory and dandelions, but covered now with brown leaves that crackled as the November breeze disturbed them.

They looked knowingly at each other as Theodore's red Chevette pulled up to the curb. Theodore was driving.

"Who invited *him?*" asked Evie with disdain.

"One *very* happy lover," said Babe in a glad tone.

Freddy ran up the steps, bringing with him a rush of lime scent. "Hi, girls," he said in his bashful way. "I hope you don't mind one more. Theodore's home."

They watched as Theodore slowly mounted the steps. He was very tall, very thin, and sported a white goatee, moustache, and slightly long white hair.

"I don't know anyone else who can climb those steps with such dignity," said Babe in a welcoming tone. She rose to hug the men.

Freddy settled nimbly on the porch rail while Theodore lowered himself tiredly to the third chair.

"Rough epic?" asked Evie sarcastically, while Babe passed the walnuts, salt, and nutcracker.

"Not an epic, but yes, very rough. My best poem ever." He had an air of heavy sincerity somewhat similar to Freddy's, but his was worldly-wise, not innocent. He wore a tweed jacket, grey wool slacks, a red sweater vest, smoked a pipe—and looked, Evie thought hostilely, a little too much like a poet was supposed to look. Still, in his presence she was more able to forgive him. He seemed to take his poetry as seriously as she took her electrical work. And he *was* president of the poetry group that met in the big church downtown and held readings she and Babe dutifully attended.

"For me!" added Freddy. "The new poem's about me."
He cracked a walnut and passed the meat to his lover.

Theodore nodded, accepting the offering, then filled
his pipe. "About Fred and myself, our life together." He
nodded again, this time toward Babe and Evie as he lit the
pipe. "And about you and you, together."

"A love poem," Freddy said in a bragging tone as he
intently explained, "but not all dressed up with big words
this time. And not about the olden days or long trips or
foreign places." A quiet wonder came into his voice. "About
growing old together and loving each other, whoever we are."

November clouds had covered the sun, and the sound of
scraping leaves made the wind seem colder. As Freddy slid
off the rail, Evie goosed him. He squealed and ran past
Theodore who stood aside in a gentlemanly way as the
others filed in.

They gathered at the table, the fragrant feast before
them. Theodore made much of each steaming dish, of the
bright white tablecloth, the highly polished silverware, the
grace of the linen napkins. Babe told them to sit while she
made still more preparations. "Are the pies in the oven to
heat?" called Evie. Freddy just ate.

"But why do you have to go away to write your poetry?"
Evie asked as Babe's deep red cranberry sauce was passed
to her.

"It won't come at home. I've tried. I've even taken days
off, staying home when Fred's at work, but end up doing
this kind of thing." He indicated the food. "Cooking great
banquets for two. Or cleaning. Or rearranging the living
room."

Freddy heaped mashed potatoes on his plate, obviously
only half listening. The scent of heating pies began to vie
with the smells of the meal. "And it's not as if I travel to the
Riviera," Theodore continued. His weary somberness began
to fade, as if he'd wrapped himself in it to protect himself

from their disfavor.

"I find the tackiest motel around," he went on, "and live in the midst of other people's squalor and drunkenness. I sleep—if I sleep—on over-washed sheets and lumpy mattresses, feed myself out of grocery bags and an electric pot I carry in my car. Often I feel like the traveling salesman in the next room, a man required by his work to displace himself, to move through worlds not his own in order to accomplish his purpose."

Sometimes Evie thought Theodore talked just because he liked to listen to himself.

Then he winked. "Except, of course, for the company those salesmen keep. Any old rough trade will do for them."

"But," Evie said, ignoring his attempt at levity and lifting the cider jug as each glass was passed to her for filling, "don't you know how miserable Freddy is?"

Freddy looked up, a startled expression replacing his passionate chewing. He'd put on a white shirt and tie for the occasion, and his cheeks were red, as if from extra scrubbing. He lovingly gazed at Theodore and explained, "I'm only miserable that he might not come home, not that he goes away."

Babe had finally stopped running back and forth between the kitchen and the holiday table. She undid her apron and finished filling her plate.

"Listen, Ev," Freddy said, wiping his mouth. "You know those little sparrows in the park?"

Evie nodded, closing her mouth on sweet buttered squash.

"How I feel about Theodore going away is like one of those little sparrows." He held his large hand over the table, palm up. "It hops on, see?" Everyone watched. "And as long as I keep my hand open, like this," he held it flat, "it stays. That's love, that little sparrow on my palm. But if I do this," he closed his fingers around the imaginary bird and made as if to squeeze it, "if I hold it too tight, it'll die."

Freddy looked across the table at his formal, fastidious lover. "After all these years I know I can't make you come back or tell you what to do when you go. All I can do is keep this hand open, and be thankful when the little bird stays."

Evie was watching the blush on Babe's face and slowly realizing that her retirement dilemma might not be all that different from Theodore's need for a separate place. Like Christmas cactuses, everyone bloomed better in her or his own hothouse. Who could say when it was time to blossom?

Babe wanted to travel—but was it the wrong season for Evie? And Babe somehow had known that if she pushed her desire on Evie, whose own personal hothouse was her little electrical shop, she might well squeeze the life from her.

By running off on his odysseys, by writing epics in grungy motels, by doing what he, not Freddy, wanted, wasn't Theodore being selfish? She herself wasn't a selfish woman—was she?

She watched Theodore pat his moustache with a napkin, elegant even while he ate, and she looked at Freddy, who, twenty minutes into the meal, still ate like a starving adolescent. She rose to pour cider all around again, silent as Theodore told traveling salesman jokes.

No, she decided. How could it be selfish for Theodore to be himself, to act like the man Freddy loved? He always did come back, didn't he? He always did run off with a poem, not a pretty young thing. That fear was Freddy's and it didn't look as if it had ever had anything to do with Theodore at all. Asking Theodore not to write poems at Thanksgiving, or any other time, was like asking the Christmas cactuses to bloom by name, not by nature.

Unexpected tears came to her eyes. She looked at the cider, wondering if it had hardened after a week on the porch. But then she realized her tears were of gratitude, for a lover who, like Freddy, cherished their love too much to try to change her. Who'd never pointed out that maybe her fear of old age creeping up and overcoming her before she'd done everything she'd wanted was making her thinking fuzzy. Who was willing to keep reading about faraway places until she could get to them. If choosing to retire wasn't selfish, after all her worrying, then she could make up her mind to do it right now.

She ate, talked, joked, and all the while thought through her dilemma. Once she felt the freedom to make her decision to retire, immediate retirement seemed less pressing. What about those compromises Babe had suggested? Leaving at sixty instead of sixty-five. Or at fifty-eight. Working just until she had enough traveling under her belt that she'd have no regrets, and Babe would get what she wanted, too. And there'd be a bigger pension, in case all those customers trickled, rather than poured, in.

At last, Freddy sat back, patting his stomach. They rose and, in playful procession, cleared the table. The cats were in the kitchen, helping themselves to everything on the counter. Freddy groaned and held his stomach as he beheld the steaming pies.

Evie folded her arms and looked sternly at him. "You don't *have* to eat my mince pie, Freddy. *Or* my fresh apple pie with cheddar cheese melted on top," she said.

A look of shock came to Freddy's face. "Are you kidding? What kind of Thanksgiving would that be, showing no gratitude to someone who can made a dessert smell like this? *And* keep a city park running single-handed if she had to."

He looked down at the oversized slab of pie she handed him. "You're not going to retire and leave me there alone for fifteen years, are you?"

"Ten," she corrected him gently. Then, without another thought, she said, "No."

She looked at Babe, who had paused, fork in midair. "No, I want it all. There'll be time to open my little shop after a few years of travel. I don't want to sit up on the Avenue looking out at all the seasons going by, wondering what they'd look like in the Petrified Forest, or San Francisco. I want more than dreams," she said, "I want memories."

Babe's mouth across the table wavered so much that Evie didn't know if she would laugh or cry. Just like last night, in the dark, Babe again said, "Ohhhh."

But it was Thanksgiving Day now, and Evie looked at Babe and then looked at Freddy and Theodore, and looked out the living room window to the sky. "Thank you," Evie said in a whisper, to no one, to everyone, the word like the bloom of a flower, welcome in any season.

JEFFERSON III:
FAMILY AND FRIENDS

The day of Gladys' funeral it was bright hot summer. But Jefferson, tall, stooping just slightly, graceful under her forty-one hard years, felt cold, so cold. She emerged from the dark subway into all that radiance hoping that the black of her pantsuit, let out at the waist since her father's funeral, would draw sunrays to her and blanket her with warm comfort. She remembered that funeral, how tranquilizers had been the wrapping around her grief till liquor was served back at the big old house she'd grown up in. She'd finally passed out on top of the guests' coats in the front room, never having shed a tear.

This church was grand, ornate. She wondered how often

Glad had set foot in it, living. Other people climbed the wide stone steps; Jefferson didn't know anyone, and hoped no one would notice Glad's lone queer friend. Customers seldom attended waitresses' funerals. There was Sam, though! Glad had worked for him half her career. Would he remember Jefferson? She'd been just another of Glad's adopted students, hanging around through college and grad school, dropping by afterward to share successes, sometimes failures. Some students returned later with pictures of their wives, husbands. Jefferson brought her lover to meet Glad, as if bringing Ginger home to mother. Some brought baby pictures. Jefferson brought winning team shots. Now and then, when she was really serious, she'd introduce a new lover. After each of these disappeared, Glad would ask, "How's Ginger?"

"Ginger's fine," she whispered now, pausing in the sunlight before mounting the steps. "Ginger's just as fine as ever, Glad," she said gratefully, feeling Glad's presence in the warmth, like a stream of herself from heaven. "She had to work today," Jefferson went on, "rehearsing her students for the big recital, but she loves you for keeping after me all those drinking years, for never letting me forget who was right for me."

She pulled the damn tissues from her pocket, remembering that Glad would always hand her napkins from a dispenser on the counter. How could she go into that cold mausoleum of a church? *I don't want you dead, Glad!* she thought, resisting with all her being. Going in there would be acceptance.

A cloud passed over the sun and then moved on, like a gentle warning. She straightened from her stoop and pushed back her short greying hair. "Okay, Glad, I get it. It's the only way I can visit you now. In sunbeams." A breeze, so seldom felt these last few days, blew at her back. She smiled. "*And* breezes." She stepped inside the church.

Her suit did hold a little warmth and she clung to it through the cool vestibule, into the still, high-vaulted church. Mourners filled the first nine rows, then straggled back to where she settled. She shuddered. Church was another place where silence was more valued than truth. Her parents would lead her there to hear the careful empty sermons as if those would teach her about life. She'd sit perfectly still, *yearning* to be outside practicing her softball pitch. "I hope you appreciate this," she teased Glad silently.

The organ began to play. There were flowers, sermons, hymns. She tried to think of Glad, to remember her, but the other mourners distracted her. She didn't want to look up at the coffin. Then someone stood up in the family pew, made his way to the front and bent to an instrument case. It was Gus, Glad's youngest, a man in a full beard now instead of a boy in a baseball cap, readying a French horn instead of a toy rifle. So Gus had become a musician. How she'd envied Glad's kids growing up with such a woman! She let her mind wander back, back to the days when they'd met.

* * * * *

The eighteen-year-old Jefferson stood at the dormitory's back door, watching her father climb heavily behind the wheel of his Cadillac. She was a freshman starting college, and her parents had driven her, with all her luggage, to school. On their way home, she knew they would stop for dinner and he would have his first drink, then a second, both doubles. He'd excuse himself and on the way to the men's room he'd quickly down another as he passed the bar. That might be enough to get him home.

Her mother ran back to the dorm to hug her one last time, clinging to this daughter she claimed not to understand. Jefferson played softball, ran, didn't date boys, didn't chatter or giggle or have long talks with mom. "What is *wrong* with you?" her mother had demanded to know, just as she'd demanded the same of her husband, but much less often and much more timorously, when the evidence of his drunkenness compelled her to confront it. Now this last buffer between herself and her husband was starting college.

Jefferson accepted the hug stiffly. What *was* wrong with her? One half of her believed in her strength and talent, and was certain of success; the other half cowered, consumed by fear and self-doubt as she listened to her mother's constant chattering about how hard she'd find college, how difficult she'd find being away from home, how ill-equipped she was for life—hard, hard life. Cowered as she watched, invisible to her parents, every nuance of every move either one made— how he drank, how she feared his drinking. Cowered as she hoped he wouldn't take another drink, and scared, so scared that when he did her mother would protest and bring on the blow-up, the confrontation. And cowered finally, in terror of her life, in the dark back seat of the car, knowing that neither she nor her mother could control their fates with Mr. Jefferson at the wheel of the box of steel, weaving his way between the white dotted lines as if they were his only guides through life. Would her mother make it home alive tonight?

"If you need to, Amelia, you can come home to us. There are lots of good schools in Westchester."

"I'll remember," she reassured her mother, wanting to scream *No! No! No!* Wanting to say, *Stop it, stop feeding my fears!*

She treasured her talented body, but her parents were suspicious of women athletes—weren't they all queer? So not only was it wrong for her to be an athlete, her error was compounded by being gay. She couldn't defend the one, or ignore the other, and she took their disapproval like blows, often longing to obliterate the body that gave her joy and yet caused her so much grief with its willful ways.

She tried to stand tall against their disapproval, against her mother's dire predictions. Still screaming inside *I'm not afraid. Why should I want to return to you?* she stared at the ground until her mother reached the car. Like her father, Jefferson would not show her fear. She would not cry. She would not even breathe. Fear could eat you alive—look at Mrs. Jefferson, too scared to leave her marriage, scared to upset her husband every minute she was in it. The heritage of her fear could eat Jefferson alive too.

The car pulled away and Jefferson waved. In a minute she would breathe. In a minute she would cry. Soon she wouldn't feel the fear. It would leave with those who'd taught it to her, who'd depended on it to keep her in line, to keep her from disrupting their lives. As the car turned the corner her father honked, twice, cheerfully free to head toward a drink. Her mother must be smothering tears, riding back toward life alone with her alcoholic, leaving behind Jefferson, her strange failure, afraid that if she cried Mr. Jefferson would only stop sooner for dinner to shut her up.

Jefferson felt as if the scream she'd muffled before was ripping from her body. A scream of protest at the life they'd go on living and that, in growing up with them, had become a part of her. A scream of abandonment. They had taught her to live in the world only as they had—how could they leave her with so little?

But she didn't scream. Or cry, or breathe much differently—or lose the fear. She felt a flash of excitement, sheer joy that she was free of them at last and she tried to give herself to it. She stood tall and moved to shrug off the fear and silence, but both had been with her much too long, and she soon felt once more the sag of her shoulders. The city roared around her like a lion after her blood. There were no sounds here of dogs barking, mothers calling. It didn't even smell like fall. That suburban life was gone and now she needed to learn new rules. She turned to enter the dorm, repeating, "They're gone. I'm free. I'm me. It's okay to play sports. It's okay to be gay. I'm going to be good at both."

Two months later, as had become her habit, she sat at the counter of a luncheonette kept prosperous by faculty and students.

"Hungover again?" The waitress, always swift and friendly, smelled of powder and cigarettes. She must have been in her mid-forties.

Jefferson nodded. Hangovers were always compounded by a return to self-doubt and an enveloping depression that left her silent and scared. She was willing to suffer them because they went hand in hand with getting high. High, she was just who she wanted to be.

The waitress slipped two aspirin next to her glass of water. Jefferson looked up in surprise, noticing that the waitress's hair had been newly permed and no longer showed grey.

"On the house," said the waitress. "After twelve years working at the College Lunchbox, I come prepared."

"Thanks," she said simply, flooded with gratitude that this woman should care. Her concern was too painful to bear. Jefferson smiled, despite her dry mouth and her insides which were sore with loneliness. Nights she drank with wise-cracking students, days she spent in anonymous lecture halls; she wasn't used to the intimacy in this waitress's eyes. Gratitude was quickly followed by fear, by a desire to run from the waitress.

She took the aspirin and swung her powerful body around on the stool to leave. Her volleyball class would start soon. Instead of hanging around the Lunchbox, maybe she'd go there early. Someone would be around to practice with, and they'd spike the ball back and forth instead of words.

When she returned to the Lunchbox a few days later, she

kept her eyes downcast to avoid the waitress's smile. She hadn't gone out drinking the night before, but she felt so down and close to tears, she wished she had. Study in the dorm made her isolation even worse. Everywhere were girls talking about their boyfriends, dates, marriage hopes. What in hell did they come to school for, when all they wanted was to find husbands?

"How are you today?" the waitress asked warmly, with real interest.

Immediately, as if she'd waited two months for just those words, Jefferson began to cry. Mortified, she turned to flee, ashamed of her weakness and the picture she must make: the crybaby jock. But the waitress blocked her way and led her to an end booth, then pulled napkins from a dispenser and offered them.

"It's hard, the work," she told the waitress, believing that that was what was wrong and blowing her nose. A nod and the warmth in those kind dark eyes urged her on. "And my friends"—she meant lovers—"are all back home. And I get teased here so much for being so . . . so unfeminine. I thought I'd like going to school in Greenwich Village"—she'd heard there were lesbians on every street corner—"but I can't meet anyone who's not an empty-headed student."

"And you miss your family?"

"No," she said, her voice bitter. "I wish I had a family I *could* miss. I'd have done anything to get away from them. Mom never wanted a jock daughter. Dad could care less."

While the waitress had to turn her attention away to serve a customer, Jefferson longed for her presence again. "Thank you," she said at her return. "I feel better." Maybe that would make the waitress stay, keep her caring.

"Bullshit," said the waitress, smiling. "But at least you opened your mouth for once. Call me Glad."

They shook hands. Jefferson loved Glad's smile so much that each time she visited her own came more easily.

"Another adopted daughter!" Sam the cook-owner said one day, shaking his head and smiling at Glad. He was six-foot-six and all the appliances in the Lunchbox kitchen were built to accommodate him. "What would you do, Glad, without your educated orphans?"

"Get a job someplace decent!"

Jefferson beamed. She felt special, privileged to be Glad's new orphan and a part of this semi-family. College began to acquire the comfort of routine. Sports brightened her days. She had found the bars where she could drink with gays at night. The morning after, Glad was usually there with that smile.

One of those mornings during her second semester, Jefferson stumbled in with a very black eye.

Glad raised an eyebrow. It was Easter vacation and her youngest, Gus, in a Yankees cap, was hanging around the restaurant shooting at customers with a toy rifle. "Out!" she told him when he'd worked himself up into a noisy frenzy. "Go shoot the tourists." He seemed to like that idea and rushed out the door. Jefferson had stayed at school for the break, to play ball, and carouse, and to avoid her parents' world. "Well?" Glad asked.

"Would you believe I got mugged?"

"No."

She'd been dreading this moment for five months. She could not truthfully explain her eye without talking about her gayness—but what good was this connection with Glad if she couldn't? She watched her clear a booth, noticed the wrinkles going deeper and deeper into Glad's skin. That touched her, Glad's age. She *couldn't* think about losing her some day. At the thought, fear, magnified by last night's liquor, grabbed hold of her.

"I got in a fight," she said impulsively. She'd learned to blot out her fear, sometimes with liquor, sometimes with recklessness. If she pushed Glad away now by coming out to her, she wouldn't have to fear losing her later. Like when she drank, there was no turning back. It was out of her hands. Was this why her father drank? She clenched her fists and plunged on. "I was drinking with Ginger. In a gay bar."

Glad didn't bat an eye.

Jefferson's smile felt like wax melted and hardened across her face. She rubbed her tight knuckles against the pale blue coffee mug. "Her old girlfriend showed up drunk. She's from the Bronx. She and Ginger ran with a rough crowd up there. The girlfriend started shouting and shoving. I told her to calm down. She's a big bruiser and before I knew it she'd popped me one."

"I hope you popped her one back," Glad said, eyes twinkling. She took one of Jefferson's hands in her own and opened it, finger by finger, till it began to relax.

Jefferson licked her dry lips, let herself breathe. "You don't care?"

"Me? Why should I care who you're screwing?"

Jefferson felt herself blush to hear it put that way, with Glad's usual bluntness. Her acceptance was so simple, like a gift; so natural, like a mother's love. But tears came to her eyes.

"Jeff, poor Sam's going to go broke supplying you with napkins."

"I *never* cry," she protested.

"You could have fooled me, kid."

After graduation, Jefferson decided to continue college for her master's degree. By that time she was bringing Glad pink roses every Mother's Day and slipping Sam a cigar with each new achievement in sports. Except for occasional drunken infidelities, she'd stayed with Ginger. Her parents paid for an apartment and she and Ginger had set up housekeeping.

"I've lived on Mott Street all my life, I *know* this city," Glad said when she brought them their housewarming present. "But I've *never* seen a place this tiny."

"My parents don't know I'm living with a girl," Jefferson said. "They think it's just my size."

Ginger laughed, hugged Jefferson with fervor. "And it *is* the size of our dorm room, plus bathroom and kitchenette. We're used to it!" She had short and bouncy red hair around a bright freckled face. Jefferson loved her dancer's legs—almost as long as her own—and her elastic body.

"Without paying rent, Ginger can afford to dance," Jefferson added, running a hand over the bouncy red hair. She mixed drinks, and then she and Ginger opened the big box together.

"A garlic press!" exclaimed Ginger.

"A spaghetti drainer!" said Jefferson.

"A cheese grater!"

"A spaghetti bowl!"

"Are you hinting that we should ask you to dinner?"

"And serve me what I'm used to," Glad replied. "I'm going to turn you into good Italian cooks!"

"Not me," said Jefferson. "I'm the bartender."

Ginger sighed. "You can teach her about wines, Glad. She hasn't passed dishwashing yet."

It was one of those jolly communal dinners when Glad announced she was going in for a mastectomy.

They were all drunk. Jefferson, her insides turned cold as her ice cubes, managed not to show her alarm and sorrow. Smoothly, but in a voice that sounded tinny in her own ears, she said, "You'll be just fine, Glad. We'll pickle you before you go in. You won't feel a thing!"

Ginger was holding the bravely smiling Glad who joked, "Ernie says he's tired of these old things anyway." Tears were falling over her smile as she outlined her abundant breasts. "He says it'll be like before the kids came, when I was a flat-chested broad." She laughed. "Just like you!"

Jefferson couldn't help but blush before that pointing finger.

Ginger held up her glass in a toast. "To all you wonderful, flat-chested broads!"

* * * * *

She shivered in the cool church all these years later, watching Gus prepare to play. Glad had come through that first operation nineteen years ago. But there had been others and Jefferson never knew, the last few years when she'd gone away for golf tournaments, alcohol cures, for the women between times with Ginger, if Glad would be at the Lunchbox when she came "home."

Yet she never went to Glad's apartment and didn't know this son who would honor Glad, nor the other children, nor Ernie. She'd felt that she wouldn't fit in on Mott Street, that the friendship couldn't be the same there. Glad had been proud to be her friend, but both of them knew that the tall dyke, greying with age, belonged just where she was in Glad's life.

Gus lifted his horn to his lips and began an excerpt from "Finlandia." She could sense Glad beaming and proud, and watching how he filled the church with breath and emotion and sound for her. She could feel her own joy at the way he returned to Glad the gift she had given him with his life.

And it took her back to her freshman self on the dormitory steps. Stricken with grief—and yes, it had been grief—to watch her own mother go, to watch her take away the gifts she'd never given, and to leave the heritage of fear. Of silence. Of alcohol.

She bowed her head, not bothering to wipe away the tears. Glad's persevering acceptance had finally sunk in. Too late for Jefferson's athletic career, but not too late to succeed at being gay. "I'm really *not* afraid to be me any more," she told the sunray stealing in through the stained glass window, and the breeze that entered when someone opened the church door. Glad and Ginger, between them, had been there when Jefferson was finally finished with drinking and on her feet again. It had been over a year now. She'd go from Glad's funeral to another AA meeting. And cry for a week if she had to.

She whispered hoarsely, "I want to cry loud enough to fill this church with sound for you."

Were tears the only gift she could give to Glad, the woman who had first loosed them? She envied the boy with his horn, who had found his own voice, and who'd had a mother who'd *heard* him all his life. But her tears would have to do: the wrong gift, to the wrong mother. And Glad would take them, as she always had.

The last of the music faded. Now, she knew, Glad felt at peace.

She left the pew, finally, but felt a hand at her elbow as she reached the church doors.

"Here," Sam the cook said, eyes wet with his own sadness. He thrust a handful of napkins toward her. "I knew she'd want me to bring some for you, too."

MARIE-CHRISTINE III:
A BUTCH NAMED DINAH

At one time in her life, Marie-Christine had been out-
rageous enough to say that she collected butches. She had
less taste now for that kind of excitement, but her relationship with Annie Heaphy allowed for an occasional impulsive
addition to the years' accumulation, and the sight of those
low green San Francisco hills after her recent slushy trek
to New York's Kennedy International stirred the old acquisi-
tive flame in her seductress's heart. Carefully she picked
her blonde curly hair and smoothed her soft white magenta-
slashed sweater. Her makeup would have to wait until she
found a stable mirror.

She hadn't been this excited about a trip since her first

visit to America at age ten. Fifteen years later, when her father had abandoned his efforts to cure her of her penchant for good-looking women and excitement at any cost, he had funded her New York boutique, as a stabilizing agent in her life. This year, business had been better, plane fares ridiculously low; and Marie-Christine had decided that it was time to see the gay capital of the world.

Now her first problem surfaced. It had taken so much time, had been so exhausting to persuade and then train the embarrassed Annie to operate the vibrator shop, that she'd completed no preparations for her trip beyond buying tickets. She needed guidance to at least get herself into the city, and none of the complications that came with asking a man.

When the passengers rose to rush from the plane, Marie-Christine spotted her solution. Was it her amazingly erect posture that made the woman stand out so? Or the thick pure-white short hair, swept back in an old-fashioned wave? She was a big woman of perhaps sixty, who wore her good looks with assurance, even dignity. A gentleman butch if Marie-Christine ever saw one. She began to hope for complications.

She came abreast of the woman in the corridor to the terminal. "Excuse me," she said in her purposefully musical French-Swiss accent.

The woman, almost her own height, smiled pleasantly, but gave no sign of recognition, no look by which to acknowledge that she noted and appreciated Marie-Christine's gayness.

Of course, thought Marie-Christine, femmes *are* harder to identify. "This is my first trip to San Francisco," she said. "I'm afraid I need some help with directions."

"I see." The woman's voice was so deep Marie-Christine wondered if she could possibly have chosen a transvestite.

But no, there was the gentlemanly courtesy: "Welcome, then, to my home town."

She looked directly into the woman's eyes, challenging her to recognize that she was a lesbian.

"You have your choice in San Francisco, dear."

Subtle, thought Marie-Christine. One certainly did have a choice in this city, if anywhere. Was this the signal? But "dear?" Not very butch. She studied her face.

"You can read some of these information machines that have replaced people," the woman said and then added, smiling, "or you can follow me."

They got their luggage and settled beside each other on a city-bound shuttle bus. The woman had lifted both their bags to the overhead rack.

"Even the airport seems different out here," commented Marie-Christine. "Hills everywhere!"

"Only your first treat," the woman assured her. "Wait until you taste the tang in the air! See the fog come in—it's our daily miracle. Look out from any hilltop window onto a scene that should only be allowed on postcards. It'll make your heart stop."

Marie-Christine turned to the woman and admired her face, patterned with very touchable-looking lines. Could she have any idea how close that face came to stopping her heart? She breathed to calm the thrill she was feeling and said, "The homes, they're like suburban tracts with a twist."

"My twisted city," said the woman proudly. "Maybe that's why I've always loved it."

Could this be another signal? Liking a twisted city?

"By the way—" said the woman.

Marie-Christine turned eagerly toward her, ready to say yes to any invitation. Oh, that gracious smile!

The woman held out her hand and said, "My name is Dinah."

Dinah? As she reached for Dinah's hand she heard a list of names in her head: Terry, Kip, Toni, Dee, Gabby, Scottie, Rickie, Nickie, Jo—but a butch named Dinah? Surely she wasn't wrong about her gorgeous guide?

* * * * *

Monday, Marie-Christine rushed into the Japanese restaurant where she'd agreed to meet Dinah for lunch. All morning she'd been thinking of this butch with the femmy name, imagining how it would be to tour the city—among other things—with her. She'd walked long, wide Valencia Street in search of its famed lesbian haunts, and visited with a sister vibrator shop nearby. This was half the reason she'd decided on San Francisco, to spend some time with another purveyor of pleasure whose clientele was intentionally female. As she walked, she breakfasted on California fruit from a variety of fruitstands, savoring its intense tastes. She couldn't get enough of it. Were native San Franciscians as much of a delight? At each corner she stopped to look up and down the roller-coaster hills lined with their colorful, intricately designed buildings as pleasing to look at as works of art.

Dinah wore a black tailored pantsuit and white blouse. She stood at the highly polished wooden sushi bar, waving, her welcoming grin as excited as Marie-Christine's felt.

"How can you *bear* to live in this incredible town?" Marie-Christine asked accusingly.

Dinah laughed, low. Her eyes sparkled as they roamed down Marie-Christine's salmon-colored, one-piece jumpsuit, tightly fitted at the waist. "You like it then, dear?"

"I *adore* it!" she replied, unable to stop her next words. "But the way you call me 'dear'—it makes you sound like an old lady!"

They'd sat down at a table, Marie-Christine almost accidentally brushing against Dinah's shoulder. She watched her face now, crazy to know for sure.

"But I *am* an old lady, dear," teased Dinah, laughing when she realized she'd used the word again. "I've just visited my newest grandchild out in St. Louis for the first time."

Marie-Christine studied the menu, concentrating on not letting her face fall, realizing that her appetite had faltered. But there were lesbian mothers galore, she reassured herself. Certainly in San Francisco. And where there were lesbian mothers, of course there would be lesbian grandmothers. *And* on all of her jaunts this morning she had not seen one woman with anywhere *near* Dinah's style. For a city where sexuality was so important, the body (and she ran her hand in a habitual gesture down her side as she thought about it) seemed very deemphasized.

In the mirror over the bar she could see that strong heavily-browed face. If she were a sculptor, she could ask for no better model. Dinah would become the archetypical guide down into the lesbian underground.

"Are all your children grown?" she asked, swiveling toward Dinah, who had just finished ordering a selection of house specialties in a knowledgeable, authoritative voice.

"Yes. All," said Dinah in a tone of exaggerated relief.

Hopeful once more, Marie-Christine sniffed a wrist to be certain she hadn't lost all of her Chanel No. 5 while traipsing around the city. "That must have been very freeing," she hinted.

"To say the least."

Their plates arrived with small mounds of pickled ginger, green horseradish and shredded turnip, the sushi banked alongside. Marie-Christine tasted each, rolling her eyes at Dinah in approval.

"Of course, when my husband died, I went and moved right in with my youngest daughter."

She could picture how Dinah had then fled this second home, maddened by the suburban conventions of the household, stalking out and heading back to San Francisco to live, finally, the life she'd always—"And do you live alone now?" she asked.

Dinah, a bit of succulent red tuna on her chopsticks, looked up, snowy eyebrows raised. "No, I still live with Jeannie."

"*Merde,*" said Marie-Christine into her tiny teacup. A lover.

"What?" asked Dinah pleasantly.

"Jeannie?"

"My daughter."

She sighed in relief, but she was getting tired of this game. She dipped a dainty makizushi in the ginger and eyed it in exasperation. It might just be her spiciest treat this trip.

But Dinah was fun, with a big rollicking laugh that rolled from her like a cable car down one of San Francisco's hills. She took Marie-Christine for a tour of the Noe Valley where she lived. They window-shopped together, tasted goodies from this shop and that, and finally rested on someone's front steps.

"I *am* sixty-three, you know," said Dinah wearily.

"No! You act my age."

"My lifestyle keeps me young. As well as my city."

"Your lifestyle?" Marie-Christine hinted, one last time.

"Leisure to do what I want. To run off on trips, spend long hours at concerts, read, squire a companionable woman around." Dinah paused as if to consider all this. "Speaking of lifestyle, would you like to do the Castro tomorrow?"

She hadn't explored this fashionable gay male ghetto yet. She accepted. Surely *this* was a signal. "Dinah," she said, quickly, before she could feel nervous, "are you gay?"

As Dinah laughed, she seemed to grow to the height of the highest city hill and her laughter to plummet down, bouncing into this narrow shaded street. "No, no, my dear," said Dinah. "Just an old Grandmom who loved her husband

and home too much to go risking it all for such frivolity as romance. One didn't, you know," she said, leaning confidentially toward Marie-Christine, "not in my day. And by the time my husband died I was too old to be chasing anyone, of any sex."

Strangely, Marie-Christine wasn't disappointed. She felt her heart thump as she asked, "You know that I am?"

There on the bright blue-painted steps, her white hair radiant under the sun which had just crept over the rooftops across the street, Dinah seemed to take her measure, boldly, with a quite stimulating effect. "I wasn't certain," she admitted. "But I thought it likely."

"And you don't mind?" she asked innocently, her mind racing to the challenge of this lesbian virgin who thought herself too old, and therefore safe from the likes of Marie-Christine the Siren.

"Mind?" Dinah laughed again, but more quietly—perhaps a little regretfully? "If I were your age. . . ."

* * * * *

She didn't plan to rush Dinah, but there was so little time left. By late afternoon Wednesday she was home from souvenir-hunting and had bathed. As she polished her nails a rich red, she planned light but beguiling makeup and a dress that would show her soft shoulders when she removed her shawl to dance. Of course, her energy might be more profitably spent by focusing her adventurously seductive spirit on a surer goal, but, she decided, winking at this pretty woman with the mischievous sparkling eyes in the mirror, what fun would that be?

It would have been as easy to meet Dinah at the restaurant, a trendy vegetarian spot decorated with hanging plants and natural wood, but she had wanted to make Dinah's role clear, at least by implication, and had asked to be picked up where she was staying. She'd taken Dinah's arm at every street corner on their way over to the restaurant. At dinner she admired the tasteful navy blue pantsuit this unlikely grandmother wore. She longed to escort her to a shop where she could buy an ascot to match the crisp man-tailored suit.

By the time they finished dinner, she'd stroked Dinah's hand enough, talked enough of the joys of lesbian love, flattered her more butchy traits enough, let her shawl slip from her shoulders enough—to know that Dinah's eyes glittered from more than the bottle of red wine they'd shared.

When Dinah proposed a walk, it was easy enough to croon, "Oh, but how I'd love to go dancing in San Francisco." She lowered her eyes and voice and asked almost shyly, "But I don't imagine you'd be willing to accompany me."

Dinah lit a cigarette. Laid a charge card over the bill. Looked at Marie-Christine and laughed once more—this time self-consciously. Had she finally lost her composure?

"You know, my charming friend, in all the sixty-three years I've lived in this town, I have never been to a gay bar."

Marie-Christine said nothing, but listened intently.

"I don't know why. Some of my husband's friends would go anywhere, do anything. I went home early more than once to avoid sightseeing in gay bars." She paused and shrugged her square shoulders. "Something in me—I don't know—it felt wrong to gawk."

Still Marie-Christine kept her silence. But she did take Dinah's cigarette from her lips, slowly, for one drag which left lipstick marks on the filter.

"And maybe I was afraid. Maybe I didn't want to see what I knew perfectly well inside. The gay life was an alternative for me. I could have been happy with a woman like you." She reddened a little. "Perhaps even happier than I was." She looked steadily across the table into Marie-Christine's eyes. "So yes. Yes, my dear. I'd like very much to go dancing with you."

"I appreciate your integrity," she replied after a silence. "I've been gawked at more than once for dancing with a woman I loved. And," she continued in a seductive rush of words, "I guarantee that you will enjoy yourself tonight."

"Maybe," replied Dinah, as they rose, "that's what I'm afraid of."

* * * * *

Marie-Christine awoke at noon the next day, stretching. With a sense of excitement she heard the phone ring and exulted at the sound of Dinah's voice.

"What a dancer you are!" she exclaimed to Dinah. Each teased the other for keeping her out till two AM. Dinah proposed picking her up again that night.

Marie-Christine leaped from her bed and dressed all in a rush. She called a cab to take her to the Purple Heart Thrift Store, a huge second-hand shop she had noticed. She'd only brought one on-the-town outfit, never expecting a long drawn-out courtship when she'd only be around a week.

The Mission District was seedy-looking. The streets were more populated than in the well-to-do parts of town. People stood in the doorways of older two- and three-story buildings, or lounged on benches and stoops. The day was overcast, but still the light seemed to glow, as if blessing a tribe which dared to build wooden homes on a faultline. Marie-Christine stepped from the cab with a sense of belonging to that tribe, of being among the zany, the determined, who valued magic light and heart-stopping hills above secure foundations. She entered the Purple Heart sure this wouldn't be her last visit to San Francisco.

Dinner, at a Wharf seafood restaurant, seemed only a preliminary. They drank white wine sparingly, as if in silent agreement that they wanted more than last night's euphoria.

It was later, while dancing at a bar, that Marie-Christine became certain she'd won her butch. She watched their reflection in a mirrored wall, Dinah slightly shorter but so broad and erect that she seemed taller than the more slender, black-sheathed woman she held. The lightness of their hair, blonde against silvery white, the way her own shoulders seemed to glow against Dinah's charcoal-grey suit and plum-colored collar. The way Dinah's hand spread over her bare back, pressing her more and more tightly. All was evidence of her progress.

"Could this be happening to me?" whispered Dinah between dances, her hot breath tickling Marie-Christine's ear.

Marie-Christine slipped a hand under Dinah's jacket, dug into her back. "I certainly hope it's you," she teased. "Because I *want* it to be you. Badly."

"There's never even been a *man* other than my husband."

"Then," she said, speaking almost against Dinah's lips, "it's about time."

She felt Dinah sway toward her, stop herself, lean again. Felt the first light touch of the tense lips, ran the tip of her tongue over those lips till they returned, full force and soft against hers, over and over.

Against them Marie-Christine said, "I have a lovely room of my own."

Dinah pulled back and stared at her as if dazzled.

"Would you like to share it with me tonight?"

* * * * *

That had been Thursday. They'd slept long into Friday morning and made love again, shades wide open, that bleached light everywhere in the room, especially on their bodies, locked together again and again. This week's wanting for Marie-Christine, and sixty-three years of wanting for Dinah, kept them in that white room above the city all day long.

By Saturday, Dinah had invited her home. Marie-Christine checked out of her hotel, thinking it strange that Dinah would want to bring her to her daughter's home for their last night. But she'd bestowed guide status on her new lover and would follow her lead. She was, she reminded herself, collecting butches.

Dinah picked her up and drove through the Presidio, up to the Golden Gate Bridge, then to the shore for Marie-Christine's first walk along the Pacific Coast. From there they went to the Japanese Tea Garden and rested in its stillness after the rush of the ocean. Dinah flavored this last stop on the tourist route as she had every other for Marie-Christine. She'd grown goddess-like in the week, taken on the aura of official Guide to the Gay City as she claimed her own place in it.

"My city," said Dinah, just before they left the Tea Garden. "I've loved it all my life, but do you know, I've never before felt its enchantment like this?"

Marie-Christine pressed against Dinah and laid her head on her shoulder.

"What I feel—is it you, or is there really something magical about being gay?"

Little waterfalls spilled from pool to pool. The sky shed light stripped of every tone but sheer white. "I don't know," Marie-Christine answered. "But in this city I'm more convinced than ever before that to be gay is to be specially blessed."

"When you were telling me how wonderful it is—to be lesbian, I admit to having listened with a grain of salt. But you were right. Maybe it has to do with accepting one's whole self. Not just the wife, but the businesswoman, the traveler, the listener, or aging woman. All the ways we might be if we were open to them."

"You are a wise guide," whispered Marie-Christine, rubbing her head against Dinah, loving her.

"You and your cuddling," Dinah said, squeezing her affectionately. "If I never kiss you again, if we never make love again, I'd settle for your cuddling."

She laughed. "You don't have to worry about getting *me* into bed again." Then she remembered where they were spending the night. "If you have privacy at home, that is."

"My daughter likes her privacy as much as I do mine," Dinah assured her, but frowned. In a moment she seemed to return from her worry. "It'll be fine," she said then, rising and grabbing Marie-Christine's hand. "Come. Let's get some dessert to bring home. Something special. This is a *big* night."

With twilight, the evening had begun to have about it an air of mystery. Was it just the wizard-like qualities with which she'd endowed Dinah? Her home was strange too, not the kind of household she'd assumed; it was a large, well-lighted, obviously newly decorated townhouse.

"This daughter, she has no grandchildren for you?"

Dinah slid the ice cream cake into its freezer and took ice from its door. "No, Jeannie's much too busy with her career."

"Hi, Mom!" Jeannie stood in the kitchen doorway, looking like a smaller-boned dark-haired version of her mother at thirty-five. Her clothes were as well-cut as her mother's, but decidedly more feminine. "Charlie won't be home right on time for dinner, but said we should go ahead."

Dinah made introductions. Jeannie looked from Marie-Christine to her mother and furrowed her brow. Why were both women acting so strangely, wondered Marie-Christine. Was Jeannie putting this visit together with her mother's absence the last two nights? It must be difficult for a straight woman to even consider that her mother might be—

At the table Jeannie and her mother began a tentative banter which sounded routine. Jeannie had just begun to question Marie-Christine about New York when the front door opened.

"That's Charlie," said Jeannie, jumping up and hurrying from the room. Marie-Christine noticed the same quality of passion caught in a smile that she'd seen in Dinah. She tried to meet Dinah's eyes, but Dinah wouldn't look up.

Then Charlie walked into the room. "Hear you've been painting the town purple with Mom," she said, offering her hand to Marie-Christine.

She heard the word purple, took one look at Charlie—stocky, with hair short in front, long in back and the walk of the Valencia Street crowd, and at Jeannie on her other arm—and threw open her arms. She saw Dinah's head snap up as she hugged Charlie, then Jeannie.

"How did you know?" asked Dinah.

Charlie laughed heartily. "Mom, we've been praying you'd see the light for *years*. And the few minutes you've been home this week all you could talk about was this new friend you'd met on the plane. Only we were afraid you were talking about a man!"

Jeannie was hugging her mother.

"Why," asked Marie-Christine of Dinah, "why didn't you tell me about Jeannie and Charlie? And tell them about me?"

Dinah's face looked torn between pleasure and extreme discomfort. "I couldn't bring myself to," she said. "The girls—what would they think, at *my* age? And you. Would you be more interested in these kids than in me once you met them?"

"Dinah, no! Ten thousand times—non, non, non," she said, covering Dinah's face, her hair, her hands with kisses.

"Marie-Christine, this blessed week you've given me was not something I wanted to share. Not right away. I didn't want to remember all the years I wasted convinced I was too old. . . ."

Charlie crossed the room and hugged them both. "We'd better sit down to dinner. If Marie-Christine's flying out tomorrow you two will have a long night ahead of you."

The grin never left Jeannie's face. "So what do you think of my mom?" she asked.

What was it the cowboys did in those American westerns? Put notches in their belts? In her mind, Marie-Christine notched her belt to mark this addition to her collection. "I think," she told Jeannie, "that your mother is one of a kind—a butch named Dinah."

A deep rumble of laughter came from Dinah. A laughter of happiness which might be echoing between the magic hills, which might be cable cars coasting down brilliant streets, atop land that trembled with life from the very center of the earth.

AT A BAR X:
HOW THEY GOT TOGETHER

There were violets, clusters of them, drooping delicately over the edges of a clear goblet on Liz's glass coffee table, their little purple petals tissue-thin velvet. Sally had arrived earlier than the rest of their friends, hoping to spend some time alone with Liz.

She touched the violets tentatively with her fingertips. "Where did you get these?"

Liz laughed low in her throat. "In the flower shop downstairs. They were a terrible splurge. I don't know what I'm going to do. Every time I pass that shop I can't keep my hands off the flowers."

Sally thought, I'll buy the shop for you. She lifted one

slender flower and lay it across her palm. It was as weight-less, as heavy, as a spirit entrusted to her. She became aware of her heart. Was it pounding? Or stopped?

Liz slid from her chair to lean against the glass table, looking up at her.

Sally looked at Liz, then at the violet in her hand. "You have a nice place here," she said, indicating the coffee table. She noticed her hand was shaking.

"Hand-me-downs," explained Liz.

But the room had become no more than background for Liz. Sally looked at the old stand-up radiator in front of the window, thinking that in winter, heat would rise off it in waves that changed everything beyond it. Lifting the violet and running it across her own cheek, she wondered if Liz was feeling what she was feeling. Or did Liz think she was a bore? And what made it like this? Why Liz? Why this room, this city, this day? Did love, like heat, rise because it had to?

She replaced the violet, her fingertips dipping into the goblet, coming out dripping. "Liz," she said, not meaning to.

"Sally," said Liz and Sally looked at her startled, like a deer surprised against the snow.

Liz's dark eyes burned behind her glasses. Her mouth—could it be swollen in anticipation?

Sally stood, walked carefully around the glass coffee table as if it were a frozen pond she might fall into. It seemed to take forever to clear. Then she folded her long legs, and dropped on top of them.

She sat facing Liz, afraid to draw breath because it might be a groan. Liz swayed toward her, head down, long dark hair hanging, her body swaying tentatively.

Sally raised one hand, then the other, until the heavy hair lay as light on her palms as the violet had. She leaned to kiss a handful of hair, leaned back again, became still, watching, waiting. Liz's eyes came slowly to hers and Sally could see the desire, the honest, clean, potent desire in them. Then she was sure of Liz, and they kissed.

They moved slightly apart when the doorbell rang. All Sally wanted in the world was to keep kissing that face, every inch of it, all the rest of her life.

But Liz rose. "They're right on time," she whispered.

When Liz swung back the door, Gabby, Bonnie and Mona, Theresa and Rickie, and Sue, were singing an old song, clapping and stomping. They immediately quieted.

Stiff with passion, Sally was unfolding her legs.

"Are we interrupting something?" asked Dixie.

Liz smiled and said nothing, gesturing them inside.

It took a moment for the group to enter, look around and relax before they regained their rowdy mood. The noise increased as Sally and Liz put on their jackets.

Simultaneously, they found excuses to go to the kitchen. They stared at each other, hesitant to grab, to press, to kiss, but desperate to somehow touch before they had to separate.

Rickie, good-looking and tanned despite the cold outside, found them like that. "Can I get a drink of water?" she asked, seemingly unembarrassed.

Liz, mute, just pointed to the sink.

While Rickie opened cabinets in search of a glass, Liz and Sally went on staring, eyes frankly exploring each curve and groove of face and neck, their hands finally reaching to touch clothes, cheeks.

"You want us to go ahead without you?" Rickie asked, watching them as she drank.

"If it wasn't Bonnie and Dixie's farewell party. . . ." Liz pulled herself away from Sally and buttoned her jacket.

Sally followed her back to the other room. Grinning, Rickie fanned her face to show their friends how things were between them.

As they left the elevator downstairs, Mona asked Sally, "When did all this start?"

"About half an hour ago," answered Sally, looking for Liz. When she found her she took her hand, looking her full in the face, purposefully revealing how this touch moved her.

* * * * *

At a bar, Gabby was telling a story. Sue, a straight girl from her shop who'd asked to come along, sat chin in hands, listening, apparently fascinated. The others drank, smoked, watched the moving crowd on the dance floor . . . except Liz and Sally, who watched each other across the table, smiling and occasionally nodding toward Gabby when they remembered to be polite.

"It's true," Gabby asserted. "The first time I saw Sal she was in a skirt."

The friends laughed. Sally shrugged toward Liz, who smiled in understanding. It was an experience common to both, wearing skirts. Their eyes shared it, the oppression of having to wear them, and the excitement of going under a skirt to touch a thigh. I'll wrap you in long purple velvet skirts, thought Sally, so you'll feel like a violet.

"And she's a mean typist," Gabby was saying. Liz looked impressed. "I can't even hit one key at a time, with these sausage-fingers." Gabby held her fingers up, then brushed ragged bangs off her pudgy face. "But Sal? When I went in there the first day her fingers were flying so fast they were a blur!"

Rickie typed across the frizzy-haired Theresa's chest until Theresa brushed her away, laughing.

Liz was staring at Sally's fingers, long and slender like her body. Sally, embarrassed, curled them into her palms, but Liz reached out like a drowning woman, and straightened them, clung to them.

"Did she sit on the boss's lap too?" big Bonnie said in

a teasing tone. She usually was the one who teased, in her deep voice.

Sally's eyes hardened and Liz glared at Bonnie.

"Sorry, Sal. I was only kidding."

"The boss was a lady, you jerk," Gabby said with a laugh.

"Wish I had a lady boss," Rickie said, motioning to the waitress to bring another round for everyone but Sally and Liz. Their glasses had sat untouched since the toast to Bonnie and Mona.

"You don't wish you had *this* lady boss," said Gabby. "At least not if she ever found out about you."

Mona wanted to know how she found out about Gabby and Sal. A P.E. teacher, she was worried about exposure.

"It was my fault," Gabby admitted, "completely."

"No." Sally wrenched her eyes from Liz. Everyone looked at her. "The Boss had a problem being who she was. You didn't. That makes it her fault."

Liz sighed, apparently at the firmness in Sally's voice. Sally heard the sigh and ran her fingers over Liz's hand.

"Her problem, my fault," Gabby compromised. "I should have stayed where I belonged."

Sue, the straight girl, was eying Liz and Sally; perhaps unconsciously, she had been adapting her posture to Liz's until her hands lay before her on the table as if waiting for Gabby's touch. "What happened?" she asked anxiously.

"See, the Boss dressed fancy. Flirted with the men bosses. Everybody thought she was *real* straight."

Gabby looked down at Sue's hands. "Like you," she said, smiling at her. When she looked up, Bonnie was winking across at Rickie as if to say, "Sure she is."

Gabby went on, "I had to wear skirts to work too. I figured I wasn't too obvious in them." The friends all giggled at Gabby, a bulldyke if there ever was one. "So when I heard about this high-class bar near where we worked, I thought

I'd drop in one night on my way home."

Theresa groaned. "You went into one of those uptown bars and thought you'd fit right in?" She always brought the group right back to earth.

Now Sue glared at Bonnie, who was laughing.

Gabby didn't seem to mind being protected. "You wouldn't believe all the women you see on the street in high heels and suits and furs and makeup who are gay! It makes me wish I could tell the whole world."

Theresa interrupted again, scowling. "They sacrifice us to stay safe in the closet themselves."

"What do you mean?" asked Sue.

"All those damn movie stars and writers and business-women. If they'd only tell the world they're gay too, we wouldn't have such a hard time." Theresa's voice was bitter.

Gabby shrugged and reached to pat Sue's hand in an affectionate way. "It's not so bad as all that."

"Yes it is," Rickie said. "Not only do straights look down on us, but the high-class gays do too."

"But being gay has its rewards," Gabby insisted, gesturing with her head toward Liz and Sally. All the friends smiled. Gabby left her hand on Sue's and Sue licked her lips as if they had suddenly gone dry.

"So," continued Gabby, "I'm sitting there watching these women at their tables and booths, wondering if I got a good job and spent all my money on clothes, could I ever be with one of them?"

"What would you want with one of *them?*" Sue asked, her eyes narrowing.

"I was younger then, and didn't know any better."

Rickie grinned at Mona who was looking at Sue's hand, still under Gabby's.

"And then the Boss walked in," said Gabby.

"Oh, no!" squeaked Sue.

Sally broke in. "You guys don't really want to hear this old story at your farewell party. . . ."

Mona waited until the waitress had served the drinks. Then she said, "Why not? First off, this is about the third farewell party you guys have set up for us. Second, I want it to be just like it always was: all of us sitting together at a gay bar, having a few drinks, a few dances, and Gabby shooting her mouth off all night!"

"Hey!" protested Gabby.

All the friends laughed again. Sally pulled Liz up with her as she said, "Speaking of dancing, and since I already *know* this particular story, I hope you'll excuse us."

"Can't hold out any longer?" Bonnie shouted after them.

Sally held Liz to her in sheer relief to be touching again. Liz seemed to melt into her. They spent half the dance standing still, looking into each other's eyes.

"I suppose we have to go back," sighed Liz as the music ended.

Sally touched her lips with her own, briefly, longingly, and they returned to their friends.

Sue watched their return, her eyes dreamily half-closed. She looked toward Gabby as if wishing she would ask her to dance.

"I wonder how long you two will last," Theresa mused aloud, not expecting an answer.

Sally smiled confidently as she sat down.

"Give them five years as good as ours," said Rickie, "and they'll be the luckiest kids in the world." Her face was flushed.

"Oh, Rick," said Theresa. "You're such a sentimentalist."

"Wish *I* had someone to be sentimental over me," Gabby sighed.

Hope gleamed in Sue's eyes. She patted Gabby's hand tentatively. "Somebody will come along," she said, beaming.

"You think so?"

Sue nodded. "Somebody who likes to listen to stories."

Rickie was nuzzling kisses all up and down Theresa's neck. "Remember when we were new?" she asked.

"Do I ever."

"I hated being new with Bonnie," Mona volunteered.

"Why?" asked Rickie.

"Because I wanted it to be all over. The passion that interfered with everything. How obsessed I was by her. I wanted to be settled down in a co-op apartment with money in the bank and a lifetime of stories to think about."

"My little old lady," Bonnie said, squeezing Mona to her.

"So here you are running off to San Francisco," Theresa said.

"We're not exactly running off," Bonnie and Mona said at once. They laughed and linked pinkies. Everyone knew they were wishing themselves luck in their new life.

Another slow song came on, but Sally and Liz didn't return to the dance floor. Instead, they moved their chairs quietly together and Liz lay her head against Sally's shoulder while Sally encircled her with an arm.

"But what happened at the high-class bar?" Sue urged Gabby.

Everyone turned to look at the bright-eyed, very young Sue. "Why don't we dance and I'll tell you?" Gabby suggested in a low voice.

"I've never heard the end either. Don't dance yet," Rickie pleaded.

Gabby fixed an evil stare on her, then turned back to Sue. "Will you dance with me after?" she asked gently.

Sue blushed. "To think this afternoon we were standing together picking and packing at the warehouse. . . ."

The friends all looked as if they were trying to hide their smiles. Gabby took Sue's hand openly now, and stroked it while Sue stared at the two hands as if she'd never experienced human touch before.

Gabby took up her story again. "At the bar, the Boss totally ignored me. But back in the office she started watching me." Sue looked concerned. Gabby smiled. "I was nervous and started making mistakes. The more she watched me, the more nervous I got and the more mistakes I made. I started drinking heavier because of the pressure. One night I drank too much and slept through the alarm in the morning. When I got to work, she was waiting for me. She let me go."

"Couldn't you appeal it?"

"There wasn't a union. Besides, I knew there was no way I could win. The most I could do was expose her to the higher bosses, but I don't believe in doing that. I'm not like the uptown queers. *I* think we have to stick together."

The waitress distributed more drinks. "But it was Sal who made all the difference," Gabby said. They all looked over to the lovers who leaned against each other, only half listening as they stroked and kissed. "I told her what happened before I left. She'd been cheering me on all along, but we weren't close or anything. All the same, you know what that big lunk did? She quit. She wrote a letter to the bosses on their own typewriter and told them off about what a good honest worker I was and walked out." There were tears in Gabby's eyes.

"Wow," said Sue, apparently ready to lay down her life for Sally, as well as for Gabby.

"So we've been tight ever since," ended Gabby.

"I never knew that part of it," Mona said in a hushed tone.

"It's just what you'd expect of Sally," Theresa said. "Those high ideals of yours. What did they ever get you?"

"Our respect," said Rickie.

Even Theresa nodded with the rest while Sally smiled.

Gabby put her arm fully around Sue. They looked like

two little bears cuddling.

"So did you get Sally and Liz together?" asked Sue.

"No," Mona answered for Gabby. "They met at our place last month."

"And haven't seen each other since then?" Gabby looked over at them, her eyebrows raised. Whispering to each other, they noticed everyone staring and broke apart.

Bonnie sighed. "I don't know if you want me to say this, Liz, but I know you wanted to call Sally so bad you scared yourself into not calling until today, when you were going to see her anyway. And from the looks of it, I'd say it was the same for Sal."

"Their saintliness is sure being rewarded tonight," Theresa commented drily.

"Good for them." Rickie squeezed even closer to Theresa. "Want to come home with me tonight, baby?" she asked her dour lover.

Gabby shrugged, as if to point out Rickie's love of a challenge. "Let's all have a dance," she suggested, looking into Sue's eyes. "It could be our last dance before you guys leave. . . ."

"I doubt it," Bonnie laughed as she and the rest of the group teased Sally and Liz onto the dance floor with them.

* * * * *

Sally saw the violets in their glass goblet first thing. Nothing had changed in Liz's living room since their friends had taken them away. Except for the white cat on the couch.

"Cheri!" Liz called in greeting, and said to Sally, "she was in the bedroom before."

Sally watched Cheri stir, then tuck her nose back under a soft white paw. "Maybe she thinks *we* might prefer the bedroom now," she suggested. A lot had passed between them since the beginning of the evening.

Liz looked at her teasingly. "And is she right?"

Sally colored, considered taking Liz in her arms, but felt shy in spite of her bold words. She shrugged.

"Would you like some coffee?" Liz asked, hanging Sally's jacket in the closet next to her own.

Sally was moved by the closeness of their clothing. "Maybe a little wine. Just to get rid of the taste of smoke in my mouth."

"If I owned a bar," Liz said as she moved toward the kitchen, "I'd say no smoking."

"You wouldn't have a bar long, then."

Liz poured red wine into a goblet identical to the one that held the violets. "Shall we join Cheri?"

They sat on the couch, to one side of the elderly cat. She opened an eye in an annoyed way.

Liz passed the goblet. Sally sipped and passed it back. This girl has style, she thought. She put one hand on Liz's thigh and began to stroke it casually.

Liz's eyes immediately glazed over. She held the goblet with two hands while Sally's fingers began to seriously caress.

Then Sally leaned to the goblet and waited for Liz to tip it toward her.

A little wine ran down her chin. She removed her hand from Liz's leg to catch it. Her glance wandered to the violets and she reached for one, this time running it gently across Liz's cheek. Liz's eyes fluttered closed.

Sally dipped the violet in the wine, then held the flower to Liz's lips. Licking off the drops of wine, Liz began, once more, to sway.

The goblet became a barrier between them. Sally dropped the single violet into the wine, then slowly, firmly, took the goblet out of Liz's hand and placed it on the table, next to the violets.

They began to move together, then stopped, as if

expecting the doorbell to ring again.

Liz whispered, "Cheri says if we're going to carry on to get the hell off her couch and into the bedroom."

Sally laughed quietly. She moved with Liz toward the bedroom, turning just once in the second before Liz touched the living room light switch.

There, in the goblets, she saw their two passions. Sally felt hers inside: clustered violets in water, ready to spill over the edge. Liz was the single intoxicating flower, floating toward her now.

JEFFERSON IV:
AROUND EVERY BASE TILL SHE WAS HOME

I'm forty-one, thought Jefferson as she watched the twenty-year-old pitcher wind up. Once *she'd* been on the pitcher's mound, her body tall, powerful, no grey in her sleek sandy hair, proud muscles in her arms. Now she was coaching. *How in hell did I get to be forty-one?*

The bat-girl trotted across the park's newly mowed grass carrying water. The hot sun felt good, heated the grass scents, made the spectators' encouragement sound languid, not demanding. Jefferson drank, remembered to smile then into those adoring bat-girl eyes. If this kid only knew, if those eyes had seen her at her depths, high on any combination of things she could get. . . .

The opponents got a hit; Jefferson tensed, ready with her signal talk to guide the Lavender Julies up the last step from their two-year slump into winning the citywide series. Her old expertise—six years of physical education training, plus all those years of playing—had never left her. Inside, she clicked, in perfect tune with her team. And they clicked with her. At last they were playing in unison, not like the beginning of the season when she'd agreed, once more, after a first year of failure and a season off, to coach the "Lavender Losers," as everyone had taken to calling them.

"You're our only hope," Sally the Bartender had pleaded for the team she and Liz sponsored.

It had been twilight outside *Cafe Femmes*. Soho was shutting down for the night. A few lingering art gallery customers sat outside sipping cafe au lait, or Irish coffee at the new sidewalk restaurant Liz had added to the bar around the time the team was born. Some of the gay kids who worked in local garment factories burst in, joking and laughing and jostling one another. Gabby was garnishing salads the customers had ordered; she had taken over the food preparation from the start, as if she'd at last found her passion in life.

Jefferson had replied, "You're pretty desperate then." She was seven months into her third attempt to live sober. Teaching again, at the prep school she'd attended as a kid. They'd taken her when no one else would give her another chance, taken her at least partly on the word of her AA sponsor, a woman who'd taught there herself when Jefferson had been the school heroine, breaking records, leading the field hockey team to victory after victory.

"Hey, hey." Gabby nudged her with an elbow as she settled her chunky body onto a stool next to Jefferson. "How's my favorite daughter of the American Revolution?"

Once something like that got out, that her family had been in New York practically since Peter Stuyvesant, she'd never heard the end of it. The kids were always kidding her about having "come out" twice. She shook her head, smiling. They liked having a fallen blue blood in their midst. Even if the blue blood could remember nothing about her introduction to society but matching chugs with her female lover, between kisses, while their male escorts waited for them outside.

"I'm under duress," Jefferson had answered, gesturing to Sally who was filling beer mugs. "I don't know if I can handle it, Gab. Coaching."

Gabby laid a hand on Jefferson's broad shoulder. "It was too much for you last time, I know." She paused. "But when you were sober, were you ever good."

As always, Jefferson's heart warmed to this praise. "Can I buy you a Julie?"

"You like my concoction," Gabby asserted. She took full credit for the drink the team was named after, although Sally had been the one who painstakingly created it to tempt Gabby away from liquor. They both watched Sally pour the grape juice and seltzer over crushed ice, and add an orange slice, a lime, a cherry. "Hey—" protested Gabby, and Sally snapped her fingers, apparently remembering only then to add another cherry. Gabby toasted Jefferson: "To a winning season."

"But I haven't said yes!"

"Listen, Jefferson," said Gabby, "it's the *Julies*. A magic team. If they win, anybody can, including you."

"What if they lose?"

Gabby looked at her appraisingly. "I'm betting you can lose one thing now without losing everything." She pulled noisily on her straw. "Customers," she had added then, bustling away to a sidewalk table.

The other team called a time out; the Julies kept their energy high, as Jefferson had taught them too, tossing the ball back and forth. She turned and saw Sally, tall, lanky,

blonde, blushing, probably at something outrageously flirta-
tious Marie-Christine, the outfielder's girl, had said. Jefferson
pictured Gabby downtown tending bar so that Sally could be
at the game. The winning game. Maybe.

She watched as three teenaged boys stopped, jeered the
teams, made clucking sounds at Marie-Christine. Jefferson's
body tensed again. Once she would have been over there in
a second, raving and raging, fists ready to repel those boys.
She turned away. Sober, she knew the team was her business.
Marie-Christine and Sally could take care of themselves.

The other team got back to work. The Julies' pitcher,
maybe drowsy from the sun, threw the batter an easy one
and the ball rose high, every head following it. The outfielder, Annie Heaphy, caught this third out and jogged nonchalantly toward home, while Marie-Christine cheered wildly,
tossing words—hero, savior, champion—like flowers toward
her.

But Annie had always been cool to work with. Even at
first, when the team had seemed to band against Jefferson,
Annie had supported her, had worked to convince the others
that Jefferson could be trusted now. Of course Annie was
new to town; Jefferson had never let her down the way she
had the others.

The way she had Ginger. Jefferson's wild Irish femme.
Red hair thick and long and wavy. Unquenchable lively
green eyes. Ginger who had always been there. In college,
where they'd first become lovers. Then those two crazy
years in graduate school when they'd lived together, full
of hopes for the future. Jefferson in the Olympics. Ginger—
well, Ginger hadn't become a famous dancer, only a dance
teacher. And the Jeffersons had locked their alcoholic
daughter in a sanitarium, hoping for a cure.

Receiving her release, thinking she was sober and fit
and raring to go again, she hadn't gone back to Ginger.
No, Ginger was behind her. Then, having recovered from a

drunken car crash, Jefferson had decided, at the age of twenty-five, to be a pro golfer. She'd be a victor again, like in college golf, like at prep school. Her parents paid for advanced instruction and financed her on the circuit where she struggled to qualify for her LPGA playing card. Where she pursued the golfing ladies, gay and straight, till the LPGA brass threatened to banish her from the tour. Her advanced age, her years out of golf, and liquor, hadn't given her much chance anyway. By the time she'd landed her most famous of the lady golfers, winning her and winning her into bed, she'd begun smoking grass, doing coke. There hadn't been a hint that she could succeed on the tour, and her parents, who were supporting her totally, gave up.

But Ginger hadn't given up. She'd been at the uptown bar, frequenting the place after dance recitals and the ballet, as if waiting for Jefferson—who sought her out, pretending not to, and had let her take her home, not letting on what she needed. That had been the second time she'd dried out. Cold turkey. Out of sheer determination. And she'd begun to teach physical education then, had stayed with Ginger eight years. During that period someone in their circle of friends had brought them to *Cafe Femmes*. Sally was an old college teammate; others in the bar remembered or had heard of Jefferson. And in the last years together Ginger would find Jefferson there, grumbling that it was the only place in the world she got respect. Ginger would call a cab—assuming she found her at all that night—and would take her home. Until one night when Ginger didn't come to *Cafe Femmes* and the next morning Jefferson found Ginger's note: *I've got to help me now. I know I can't be with you till you do something for yourself.*

The women at *Cafe Femmes* had watched all that. Some had been on the softball team that first year when Jefferson, still drinking, had failed them so badly as a coach. Not a few had fallen for the still-powerful Jefferson and had hoped to win her from the memory of Ginger, had tried to cure her addictions—and had ended up being hurt themselves.

It was Ginger who still had Jefferson's college cap. The cap that had, at least partially, drawn Jefferson back to the woman who'd kept and treasured a hat worn during the winning of so many games. Sometimes it seemed as if that cap and Ginger's memories were all that was left of Jefferson's glory.

Shielding her eyes with one hand, she watched the Julies get a hit, a strikeout, a walk. They'd learned to trust her, despite the way she'd been. They'd learned, too, what she'd taught. And they were up a long time before the umpire called Millie out on strikes. But they hadn't gotten a run. The score was two to two.

"You're good, coach," Annie said as she prepared to jog to her position in the outfield.

"Thanks, Heaphy." But what, Jefferson wondered, am I doing here at forty-one, coaching a dinky little amateur softball team? What in hell did it matter if *they* won or lost?

Out of the corner of her eye she saw Liz arrive. Sally's partner at the bar and at home, Liz worked the night shift. She must have just gotten out of bed. She reminded Jefferson of Ginger: tough, but devoted to her woman and her dream. She'd told Jefferson that she saw *Cafe Femmes* as much more than a gay bar, as a place where gay kids could be together whether they drank or not. She watched Liz and Sally hug, smile into each other's eyes. Their passion just never seemed to die, thought Jefferson admiringly as she turned back to the game. Like hers for Ginger. If only she hadn't treated her so badly. Twice. In AA, they said don't start a new relationship in the first year of sobriety. But she didn't want a new woman, she wanted the warmth and comfort of Ginger. And not because she knew her from back when. She wanted to be worth something to Ginger now.

She could see Liz watch the game intently, holding Sally's hand. It mattered to Liz that the Julies won. That night last summer, after Ginger had left, when Jefferson had been the only one in the bar, and Liz had apparently thought she was too drunk to notice—how could she ever forget that night? It came back to her vividly.

Behind the bar Liz had been sobbing in Sally's arms. No-nonsense Liz, sobbing. She could see Sally's hand stroke Liz's thick dark hair.

"We can borrow more money," Sally had been saying.

"No," Liz had mumbled. "We're not going under because of my dreams. Look what happens," she'd said, gesturing toward Jefferson.

With no one else there, *Cafe Femmes* had felt like a cold cave. The jukebox had been silent; the electronic game, like some night bird, beeped only occasionally; there were no sounds from outside. There was no place in the world but this refuge and its darkness had seemed to thicken before Jefferson's eyes, shadows gathering to blot out her life, her world.

"The bar is still healthy," Liz had gone on, drying her eyes. "I won't sacrifice it for some iffy sidewalk cafe the kids might not even come to." She leaned against Sally. "Half a dream's better than none, right?"

"Wrong," Sally had said quickly. "We'll make it."

"How?"

"Faith. You believe in what we're doing. I believe in it. We have to have some faith that our instincts are right, that this is exactly the right time for a space where gays and straights can mix. The right place for a gay bar the neighborhood can be proud of."

Liz's tone had been bitter. "Even the Lavender Julies can't win."

"Yet. They're only three years old."

Liz laughed through her tears. "You're a hopeless

optimist." She blew her nose.

"Not hopeless," Sally said. "You know, I always thought we had to hide away in a dingy neighborhood, come and go in the shadows. I never expected Soho to take off like this. And you taught me to hold up my head here. To put that fancy lavender awning out front. To spill our dirty gay selves onto the sidewalk. To get those blatant lavender and red uniforms for the Julies." She pulled Liz close. "*You*, baby. Maybe the neighborhood's not bragging about us yet, but *I* feel better. The kids do too."

But Liz had been looking at Jefferson. "They do? They sure don't bother to show it."

Had it been that night, that very moment, Jefferson wondered now in the light of a new day, that she'd begun to fight her way up? Dreams, she thought now, as the Julies fought not to lose. Dreams. She savored the word in the bright daylight, as coach of this bright lavender and red team. Every woman out there was dreaming of winning, just as she once had. And for all her awards, had she really ever won yet? Won like Sally meant when she spoke of Liz's dream? Win something for herself by winning for everyone? *Was* this a dinky little team she coached? Hell no. She'd learned what *they'd* taught her, too. They were quick and smart, skilled now, she'd made sure of that. All they'd needed was a leader. And what did their leader really want? To be a sad has-been all her life? Or to give them something to hold their heads up for?

She watched the batters on the other team more closely. The one up now would freak out at a curve ball, she decided, and signaled the pitcher to throw one. As the pitcher struck her out, Jefferson saw it all in her mind's eye: the Julies, in bright red and proud lavender, at the street fair next month, behind the *Cafe Femmes* booth, under a big sign: ALL-CITY WINNERS! The Julies, shaking cans at people to collect funds for block improvements, block gatherings, for pro gay political candidates who wanted the Soho vote. Legalize lofts! They'd carry the red and lavender banner through the streets, representatives of the community. And on Gay Pride Day they'd march, they'd parade, they'd storm the city, waving at the cameras. Shadows? Never again, Sal and Liz! They'd *lead* the damn parade, triumphant, all-star champs: the players and their lovers, fans, mothers, fathers— their coach. Yes, she could use a little glory, too. Not glory like it used to be but, shit, who remembered that now? Except herself. Except Ginger.

It was the last half of the last inning. Annie Heaphy stepped up to bat. The teams were still tied. The sun was a little less hot. The grass was strewn with intent lesbians. Even the teenaged boys, passing back through, seemed gripped by the tension. Marie-Christine had begun a cheer:

Our
Lavender Lovers
Are
Lavender Winners!

Jefferson remembered the very first time her own team had won, they'd been playing field hockey up in Rye. She was very together, in tune with her teammates, and had pushed and wheeled her way toward the winning point. The cheers sounded—the cheers that were, for that glorious moment, the only sound in the world.

She'd thought she'd never hear them like that again and here they came now, rising, swelling as Annie Heaphy hit the ball with all the power in her forty-year-old arms and it sailed over the pitcher, sailed over second base, sailed over the outfield, toward the roof of the Plaza Hotel and Annie came running, running, no longer nonchalant, around every base till she was home. Home.

Jefferson didn't care who saw her. She stood crying in

front of everyone. Crying to see the bat-girl twirl in excitement, to see Liz smiling and crying all at once, to see Sally leaping with delight, to see Marie-Christine dance Annie around and around.

To see Ginger.

Where had she been? Watching out of sight?

And holding Jefferson's cap. Her winner's cap—looking faded, worn, but with a good stiff brim to it still, bent in the middle, just where she liked it.

"I thought you might need this again," said Ginger, tears glistening in those green eyes that looked like home.

Jefferson bypassed the hat, opened her arms. Ginger stepped in. The cheers still filled Jefferson's ears.

A few of the publications of
THE NAIAD PRESS, INC.
P.O. Box 10543 • Tallahassee, Florida 32302
Mail orders welcome. Please include 15% postage.

THE LOVE OF GOOD WOMEN by Isabel Miller. 224 pp. Long-awaited new novel by the author of the beloved *Patience and Sarah.*   ISBN 0-930044-81-9 $8.95

THE HOUSE AT PELHAM FALLS by Brenda Weathers. 240 pp. Suspenseful Lesbian ghost story.   ISBN 0-930044-79-7   7.95

HOME IN YOUR HANDS by Lee Lynch. 240 pp. More stories from the author of *Old Dyke Tales.*   ISBN 0-930044-80-0   7.95

EACH HAND A MAP by Anita Skeen. 112 pp. Real-life poems that touch us all.   ISBN 0-930044-82-7   6.95

SURPLUS by Sylvia Stevenson. 342 pp. A classic early Lesbian novel.   ISBN 0-930044-78-9   7.95

PEMBROKE PARK by Michelle Martin. 256 pp. Derring-do and daring romance in Regency England.
                                      ISBN 0-930044-77-0   7.95

THE LONG TRAIL by Penny Hayes. 248 pp. Vivid adventures of two women in love in the old west.   ISBN 0-930044-76-2   8.95

HORIZON OF THE HEART by Shelley Smith. 192 pp. Sizzling romance in summertime New England.
                                      ISBN 0-930044-75-4   7.95

AN EMERGENCE OF GREEN by Katherine V. Forrest. 288 pp. Powerful novel of sexual discovery.   ISBN 0-930044-69-X   8.95

THE LESBIAN PERIODICALS INDEX edited by Claire Potter. 432 pp. Author and subject index.
                                      ISBN 0-930044-74-6   29.95

DESERT OF THE HEART by Jane Rule. 224 pp. A classic; basis for the movie *Desert Hearts.*   ISBN 0-930044-73-8   7.95

SPRING FORWARD/FALL BACK by Sheila Ortiz Taylor. 288 pp. Literary novel of timeless love.   ISBN 0-930044-70-3   7.95

FOR KEEPS by Elisabeth Nonas. 144 pp. Contemporary novel about losing and finding love.   ISBN 0-930044-71-1   7.95

TORCHLIGHT TO VALHALLA by Gale Wilhelm. 128 pp. Classic novel by a great Lesbian writer.   ISBN 0-930044-68-1   7.95

LESBIAN NUNS: BREAKING SILENCE edited by Rosemary Curb and Nancy Manahan. 432 pp. Unprecedented auto-biographies of religious life.   ISBN 0-930044-62-2   9.95

THE SWASHBUCKLER by Lee Lynch. 288 pp. Colorful novel set in Greenwich Village in the sixties.   ISBN 0-930044-66-5   7.95

MISFORTUNE'S FRIEND by Sarah Aldridge. 320 pp. Historical Lesbian novel set on two continents.
                                      ISBN 0-930044-67-3   7.95

A STUDIO OF ONE'S OWN by Anne Stokes. Edited by
Dolores Klaich. 128 pp. Autobiography. ISBN 0-930044-64-9   7.95

SEX VARIANT WOMEN IN LITERATURE by Jeannette
Howard Foster. 448 pp. Literary history. ISBN 0-930044-65-7   8.95

A HOT-EYED MODERATE by Jane Rule. 252 pp. Hard-hitting
essays on gay life; writing; art.   ISBN 0-930044-57-6   7.95

INLAND PASSAGE AND OTHER STORIES by Jane Rule.
288 pp. Wide-ranging new collection.   ISBN 0-930044-56-8   7.95

WE TOO ARE DRIFTING by Gale Wilhelm. 128 pp. Timeless
Lesbian novel, a masterpiece.   ISBN 0-930044-61-4   6.95

AMATEUR CITY by Katherine V. Forrest. 224 pp. A Kate
Delafield mystery. First in a series.   ISBN 0-930044-55-X   7.95

THE SOPHIE HOROWITZ STORY by Sarah Schulman. 176
pp. Engaging novel of madcap intrigue.   ISBN 0-930044-54-1   7.95

THE BURNTON WIDOWS by Vicki P. McConnell. 272 pp. A
Nyla Wade mystery, second in the series. ISBN 0-930044-52-5   7.95

OLD DYKE TALES by Lee Lynch. 224 pp. Extraordinary
stories of our diverse Lesbian lives.   ISBN 0-930044-51-7   7.95

DAUGHTERS OF A CORAL DAWN by Katherine V. Forrest.
240 pp. Novel set in a Lesbian new world. ISBN 0-930044-50-9   7.95

THE PRICE OF SALT by Claire Morgan. 288 pp. A milestone
novel, a beloved classic.   ISBN 0-930044-49-5   8.95

AGAINST THE SEASON by Jane Rule. 224 pp. Luminous,
complex novel of interrelationships.   ISBN 0-930044-48-7   7.95

LOVERS IN THE PRESENT AFTERNOON by Kathleen
Fleming. 288 pp. A novel about recovery and growth.
                                          ISBN 0-930044-46-0   8.50

TOOTHPICK HOUSE by Lee Lynch. 264 pp. Love between
two Lesbians of different classes.   ISBN 0-930044-45-2   7.95

MADAME AURORA by Sarah Aldridge. 256 pp. Historical
novel featuring a charismatic "seer."   ISBN 0-930044-44-4   7.95

CURIOUS WINE by Katherine V. Forrest. 176 pp. Passionate
Lesbian love story, a best-seller.   ISBN 0-930044-43-6   7.95

BLACK LESBIAN IN WHITE AMERICA by Anita Cornwell.
141 pp. Stories, essays, autobiography.   ISBN 0-930044-41-X   7.50

CONTRACT WITH THE WORLD by Jane Rule. 340 pp.
Powerful, panoramic novel of gay life.   ISBN 0-930044-28-2   7.95

YANTRAS OF WOMANLOVE by Tee A. Corinne. 64 pp.
Photographs by the noted Lesbian photographer.
                                          ISBN 0-930044-30-4   6.95

MRS. PORTER'S LETTER by Vicki P. McConnell. 224 pp.
The first Nyla Wade mystery.   ISBN 0-930044-29-0   7.95

TO THE CLEVELAND STATION by Carol Anne Douglas.
192 pp. Interracial Lesbian love story.   ISBN 0-930044-27-4   7.95

THE NESTING PLACE by Sarah Aldridge. 224 pp. Historical
novel, a three-woman triangle.   ISBN 0-930044-26-6   7.95

THIS IS NOT FOR YOU by Jane Rule. 284 pp. A letter to a
beloved is also an intricate novel.   ISBN 0-930044-25-8   7.95

FAULTLINE by Sheila Ortiz Taylor. 140 pp. Warm, funny,
literate story of a startling family.   ISBN 0-930044-24-X   6.95

THE LESBIAN IN LITERATURE by Barbara Grier. 3d ed.
Foreword by Maida Tilchen. 240 pp. A comprehensive
bibliography. Literary ratings; rare photographs.
                                       ISBN 0-930044-23-1   7.95

ANNA'S COUNTRY by Elizabeth Lang. 208 pp. A woman
finds her Lesbian identity.   ISBN 0-930044-19-3   6.95

PRISM by Valerie Taylor. 158 pp. A love affair between two
women in their sixties.   ISBN 0-930044-18-5   6.95

BLACK LESBIANS: AN ANNOTATED BIBLIOGRAPHY
compiled by J.R. Roberts. Foreword by Barbara Smith. 112
pp. Award winning bibliography.   ISBN 0-930044-21-5   5.95

THE MARQUISE AND THE NOVICE by Victoria Ramstetter.
108 pp. A Lesbian Gothic novel.   ISBN 0-930044-16-9   4.95

LABIAFLOWERS by Tee A. Corinne. 40 pp. Drawings by the
noted artist/photographer.   ISBN 0-930044-20-7   3.95

OUTLANDER by Jane Rule. 207 pp. Short stories and essays
by one of our finest writers.   ISBN 0-930044-17-7   6.95

SAPPHISTRY: THE BOOK OF LESBIAN SEXUALITY by
Pat Califia. 2d edition, revised. 195 pp.   ISBN 0-930044-47-9   7.95

ALL TRUE LOVERS by Sarah Aldridge. 292 pp. Romantic
novel set in the 1930s and 1940s.   ISBN 0-930044-10-X   7.95

A WOMAN APPEARED TO ME by Renee Vivien. 65 pp. A
classic; translation by Jeannette H. Foster.
                                       ISBN 0-930044-06-1   5.00

CYTHEREA'S BREATH by Sarah Aldridge. 240 pp. Women
first entering medicine and the law: a novel.
                                       ISBN 0-930044-02-9   6.95

TOTTIE by Sarah Aldridge. 181 pp. Lesbian romance in the
turmoil of the sixties.   ISBN 0-930044-01-0   6.95

THE LATECOMER by Sarah Aldridge. 107 pp. A delicate love
story set in days gone by.   ISBN 0-930044-00-2   5.00

ODD GIRL OUT by Ann Bannon   ISBN 0-930044-83-5   5.95
I AM A WOMAN by Ann Bannon.   ISBN 0-930044-84-3   5.95
WOMEN IN THE SHADOWS by Ann Bannon.
                                  ISBN 0-930044-85-1   5.95
JOURNEY TO A WOMAN by Ann Bannon.
                                  ISBN 0-930044-86-X   5.95
BEEBO BRINKER by Ann Bannon   ISBN 0-930044-87-8   5.95
     Legendary novels written in the fifties and sixties,
         set in the gay mecca of Greenwich Village.